THE SPIRIT HOUSE

WILLIAM SLEATOR

THE SPIRIT HOUSE

WILLIAM SLEATOR

DUTTON CHILDREN'S BOOKS
NEW YORK

The author wishes to acknowledge

Surachest Chum-Up
Chrea Sek
Lynette Feather-Hatton

for their invaluable help with this book.

Copyright © 1991 by William Sleator

All rights reserved. No part of this publication may be reproduced or transmitted in any form or by any means, electronic or mechanical, including photocopy, recording, or any information storage and retrieval system now known or to be invented, without permission in writing from the publisher, except by a reviewer who wishes to quote brief passages in connection with a review written for inclusion in a magazine, newspaper, or broadcast.

Library of Congress Cataloging-in-Publication Data

Sleator, William.
     The spirit house / William Sleator.
          p. cm.
     Summary: Fifteen-year-old Julie investigates the suspicious behavior of the Thai exchange student staying with her family and comes to believe in the wish-granting power of a spirit that appears to have followed him across the ocean.
     ISBN 0-525-44814-4
     [1. Supernatural—Fiction.   2. Mystery and detective stories.] I. Title.
PZ7.S6313Sp   1991   91-2131
[Fic]—dc20   CIP
                                            AC
Published in the United States by Dutton Children's Books, a division of Penguin Books USA Inc.
375 Hudson Street, New York, New York 10014

Editor: Ann Durell   Designer: Joseph Rutt

Printed in U.S.A.   First Edition   10 9 8 7 6 5 4 3 2 1

For Paul

1

"I bet what's-his-name believes in spirits. Everybody in Thailand believes in spirits," said Dominic, my eleven-year-old brother.

"Don't exaggerate, Dominic," Mom told him. "It's a modern country. It must be only the uneducated people in little isolated villages who still believe in things like that."

"Nope," Dominic said, balancing his fork on the end of his finger. He was excited about the foreign student from Thailand who was coming to live with us, and in his usual thorough way, he had been doing research. "Educated people, professors, scientists, they all believe in spirits. They even make deals with them. They'll ask a spirit to do something for them and promise to pay the spirit back if it helps them, by giving jewelry or money to the spirit's shrine. And then if they get what they asked for, and *don't* pay the spirit back, they're really in trouble."

"*Professors* believe in that kind of thing?" Dad said doubtfully.

"Yes," Dominic insisted, jiggling his finger just enough to rock the fork without upsetting its balance. "And everybody has these little structures called spirit houses, outside their real houses, and even outside office buildings and banks and things. So the spirits will go live in them, instead of bothering people inside. I can show you pictures."

"I'm sure it's just some sort of vestigial cultural thing," Mom said. "He'll explain that to you when he gets here."

"He" referred to the foreign student, whose name, Thamrongsak Tan-ngarmtrong, was so unpronounceable that we all felt a little self-conscious about saying it. Mom and Dad had found him through some university connections of Mom's—a good student, but from a poor family.

"I wonder," Dominic said thoughtfully, his attention wandering away from the fork. "Do you think he'll be worried about spirits bothering him because *we* don't have a spirit house?" The fork clattered onto his plate.

Dad laughed. "I'm sure he'll have lots of other things on his mind."

I was fifteen, and, unlike Dominic, I wasn't thrilled, to put it mildly, by the idea of having this foreign student come and live with us. I was sure it would wreck my sophomore year. We had moved to this neighborhood when I was a freshman, I hadn't known any of the kids at school, and it was only at the end of the year that I had become part of a group and had started going out with Mark. He was popular and good-looking enough to help my status, but I wasn't really secure—the kids were very socially competitive. And Mark had been away for a month on a trip to Europe. He'd written me several postcards; I hoped that meant we were still going to-gether.

But it wouldn't help my social life to be saddled with some weird little Asian guy. I knew Mom would expect me to include him in everything, which would probably mean I'd end up being left out. When I mentioned the foreign student to my best friends, Gloria and Lynette, they immediately started making jokes about his name.

Mom kept saying it was petty and selfish of me to make any objection to helping an underprivileged person from a developing country. When she talked about how it was our duty to share what we had with someone less fortunate, I gagged.

She yelled at me, "He's coming, Julie, and you'll go out of your way to be nice to him—period!" and I ran up to my room and slammed the door and tried to tell myself that he *might* not be so bad, after all.

Then we got his neatly handwritten letter. The English was excellent, but the content was pathetically earnest. Mom and Dad enjoyed the parts about how grateful he was to them, his "most kindly benefactors," and how important this experience would be for his future. He also wrote about his fascination with math and foreign languages and said, "When not at school or working I spend all my time on my studies and have no time for wasting on movies, television, pop music, or dancing."

Then he went drippily on and on about how the most important thing in his life was fulfilling his duty to his beloved parents and grandparents and ancestors, and to the Lord Buddha.

But he didn't only *sound* like a jerk. There was also a photograph, which confirmed my worst fears. He was

3

literally shaven bald, with a lumpy head and big ears and a deadly solemn expression on his narrow, sallow face. My only hope was that he would somehow manage to find a few other nerds like himself to hang out with. I began making mental lists of social outcasts at school to whom I could introduce him as quickly as possible.

He arrived a week before school started. Mom insisted that I go with them to meet him at the airport. I argued and sulked about it, but I had no excuse not to go. And I *was* vaguely curious.

We stood self-consciously at the international terminal, Dad holding up the long piece of cardboard on which Dominic had managed to squeeze the word "Tan-ngarm-trong." I felt more and more depressed as we watched the Asian passengers emerge from customs.

There were some in groups who looked like refugees, wearing cheap clothes that did not fit, clustered together as they gazed around. Others, very well-dressed, were blasé, as though they had made the trip many times before; these passengers seemed to keep deliberately well away from the refugees. One handsome Asian jet-set couple strolled quite close to us, smoking cigarettes and chatting amiably. There was not a rumple or a crease between them; you never would have guessed they had just stepped off a twenty-four-hour flight. My eyes were naturally drawn to them, in the wistful way that one gazes covertly at beautiful people from an unattainably glamorous world.

We waited. Fewer people were coming out now. Mom and Dad began to worry—and I began to hope—that Thamrongsak had missed the plane. There was nobody who in any way resembled the photograph.

Then Mom gestured at a shabby boy in thick glasses just coming dazedly through the door. "Look, I bet that's him! Maybe we should . . ." Her voice died as an elderly Asian man rushed to embrace him.

I sighed and glanced again at the elegant couple. They both wore the kind of clothing and gold jewelry you see in expensive magazine ads. Both were good-looking, especially the tall young man, who had high cheekbones and a strong chin and a thick shock of dark hair that tumbled over his forehead. He wore a loose gray open-necked silk shirt and a beautifully fitted black suit.

And then he shook hands with the woman and turned and strolled toward us, his posture erect yet relaxed. "Mr. and Mrs. Kamen, really happy to meet you," he said smoothly. He lifted his hands, his palms pressed together in a kind of praying gesture, and slightly lowered his head.

It took me a very long moment to begin to grasp the concept that *this* must be our foreign student. And as the astonishing fact slowly sank in, I also realized that he had seen our sign from the beginning, because of the way he'd walked directly toward us now, without looking around at anyone else. Absorbed in conversation with his wealthy fellow passenger, with whom he seemed to have become very friendly, he had simply taken his time about coming to greet us.

We were all a little nonplussed, and I felt more shy than I had in years. Mom and Dad kept looking at each other on the way to the car as they asked him questions, while Dominic and I took turns carrying his suitcase.

Mom did not seem all that pleased about Thamrong-sak's unexpected sophistication and good looks. I knew she had been looking forward to some poverty-stricken, scholarly, awkward guy who would be humbly and excessively grateful for our tremendous life-changing benevolence to him. Instead she had been dealt this self-confident man of the world. The irony was beautiful to behold—given what Mom had *thought* she was going to be inflicting on me. It was all I could do not to chuckle out loud.

Mom had to tell Thamrongsak to wear his seat belt—apparently they didn't have them in Thailand, and though Thamrongsak was willing to oblige her, he had a little trouble fastening it. And then he actually put a cigarette in his mouth and pulled a gleaming gold lighter from his pocket. When Mom told him there was no smoking in the car he murmured an apology and immediately clicked off the lighter. But what was he going to do about the fact that there was also no smoking in the house? This was going to be interesting.

I watched him put the unlit cigarette back in his shirt pocket. And I noticed a jade pendant on a heavy gold chain around his neck. The carving was very delicate; I had never seen anything like it.

I was the one who had the nerve to bring up the question we were all wondering about. "How come you looked so *different* in the picture you sent us?" I asked him.

"Picture?" he said, stiffening slightly.

"Picture. That means photograph," Dominic explained. "You were bald and wearing a robe like a Buddhist monk."

"Oh, yes, photo," Thamrongsak said, relaxed again. "Make photo last day of being monk in *wat*."

He didn't seem to want to say any more about it, but Mom and Dad and Dominic pelted him with questions. Very gradually the information emerged that it was a normal part of Thai culture for all young men to spend a few weeks or months living in a *wat*, or temple, as Buddhist monks. Their heads were shaved, they wore saffron robes, they spent their time praying, studying, and begging for alms. Their diet consisted mainly of whatever scraps people happened to drop into their alms bowls in the morning, which they *had* to eat, however stale and unappetizing. "Old story of very holy man. Thumb of leper fall into bowl—and he eat it," was the one piece of information that Thamrongsak volunteered without it having to be pried out of him.

"Did *you* ever eat a leper's thumb?" Dominic asked him, obviously impressed.

"I don't *think* so," Thamrongsak said, with a half smile.

Under further questioning, he admitted that he had chosen to stay with the monks in the temple a good deal longer than the minimum time required. That was why he had grown so thin and looked so different in the picture. Mom seemed somewhat mollified by this evidence of Thamrongsak's seriousness and piety: *this* was more like the kind of person she had had in mind.

Dad carried the suitcase from the car and Mom unlocked the front door. Thamrongsak slipped off his shoes as we stepped inside the house—and before the door was even shut he was already puffing on a cigarette.

Mom set down her handbag on the hall table and turned back to Thamrongsak. "Welcome to your new—"

she started to say. And then her lips tightened. "I guess we didn't make it clear in the car, Tham—Thamrongsak," she said, making an effort to sound firm while stumbling over his name—it was the first time any of us had dared to say it in front of him. "We have a rule here. There is no smoking in this house."

"Please. Not say Thamrongsak. That formal name," he told her. "Good friend call by nickname, Bia."

That was a relief; "Bia" was a lot easier to pronounce. But Mom didn't relax. "All right then, *Bia*," she said. "But there is no smoking in this house."

Bia looked at our feet. "Is American custom, like wearing shoe inside house?"

I watched Mom's face, once again feeling the impulse to giggle. "It's a custom in *this* house," she said.

"Really sorry," Bia said, very apologetic now. He quickly slipped on his shoes and disposed of the cigarette outside.

He started to take off his shoes again when he came in, but Mom assured him that it *was* an American custom to wear shoes inside the house, so he left them on. He nodded politely as we trooped around showing him the living room, dining room, kitchen, and family room before taking him upstairs. "Nice house" was all he said. Mom kept flashing looks at Dad. She would have preferred him to be awed by the spacious luxury of our comfortable middle-class home.

Then we took him upstairs to the guest room. The smallest bedroom, it had a single bed, a bookcase, a closet, and a small desk. It was nothing special, but pleasant enough, and Mom and Dad had provided the desk and new curtains especially for Bia. Mom had probably been hoping he would gush about how he had always slept with ten brothers and sisters and had never had his own room before. But he merely nodded pleasantly. "Thank you," he said. "Nice room."

"I bet you want to get cleaned up and settled in after your long flight, don't you? You know where the bathroom is. Come on, Julie, Dominic," Dad said, beginning to herd us away. Bia bent his head and made the praying gesture, and Mom closed the door behind her.

For a long moment we remained in the hallway, silently looking at his door.

"Why are we all just standing here?" I suddenly said, breaking the spell. Dominic hurried up to the third floor to his room and his computer, and Mom and Dad, looking thoughtful, went downstairs.

As soon as they were all out of the way, and I was sure I wouldn't be noticed, I ducked into Mom's second-floor study, where Bia's papers were kept. I still couldn't get over how unexpectedly good-looking he was, how different from the photograph he had sent, and I got out the photo and studied it carefully. It didn't *seem* to look much like him, though it was hard for me to tell for sure, because I didn't know many Asians, and to my Western eyes Asians had similar features. The guy in the picture did have the same high cheekbones and flattish nose. And who else could it be, anyway? But I was still amazed by what a difference no hair and a ten-pound weight loss could make. Mom probably wished he *still* looked like the picture. I smiled at that thought.

Then I glanced up and saw Bia standing in the hallway, watching me. He was wearing a dark blue robe, but the green pendant was still around his neck.

I blushed and put the photo down, as though I had been caught spying.

Bia started to move toward me. We heard footsteps on the stairs. He turned away and walked silently past the doorway.

2

It took Bia a full hour to shower and change. When he finally came downstairs I was in the family room with Dad, watching a baseball game on TV. Bia was wearing black linen pants and a fresh red and black cotton shirt, loosely fitted, which looked great on him.

After making the little praying gesture to Dad, he sat down and lit a cigarette.

Had he already forgotten the scene with Mom? "Come on, you better do that outside," I said. I opened the sliding glass doors that led from the family room out onto the backyard deck. Bia followed me down onto the lawn. "Cigarette?" he offered, taking the pack from his shirt pocket.

I shook my head. "Bia, do you have a lousy memory or what?" I said.

"Memory? I forget something?" Once again, he seemed to stiffen slightly.

"I mean about smoking. Don't you remember Mom making you do it outside?"

"Oh. Only forget about smoking," he said, and shrugged, as though it had been just a small oversight.

"Look, Mom's real intense about it. If you want to get along with her, don't smoke in the house."

"Yes, I remember now. Thank you, Julie, for help with parent, and with American custom," he said, very gravely and sweetly. "I really *appreciate*." He could barely pronounce the word.

Though Bia wasn't the humble, self-effacing type we had expected, he was unfailingly polite to Mom and Dad. Often he would *wai* to them—that was the little praying gesture of greeting, which he explained was only done to those of superior status, a sign of respect. And respectful he certainly was. He would not speak to Mom or Dad until spoken to, would not mention anything he needed until specifically asked.

Nor would he volunteer any personal information. It was almost impossible for Mom and Dad to wrest from him any specific details about his family or his school or his friends. At supper, when Dad asked him what he did for recreation, he shifted the subject to sports in Thailand—he had learned quickly what Dad would be interested in. When Mom asked him about his mother, he brought up the independent role of women in Thailand, exactly the topic that would please Mom—and distract her from asking him more personal questions.

When Dominic and I finished the supper dishes we found Bia in the family room, watching a stupid game show with great fascination.

"You want to play this really cool math game I have on my computer?" Dominic asked him.

"Thank you. Not now," Bia said, his eyes glued to the TV.

"But in your letter you said you liked math," Dominic said.

"Letter?" Bia asked him, turning from the TV screen with a blank expression.

"Yes, your letter. You said you loved math and foreign languages and didn't like movies and television," Dominic prodded him. "Don't you remember *that?*"

"I remember," Bia said. He looked away, as though distracted by his reflection in the glass door, his back very straight. "Only is . . . sometime, if I . . ." He turned to Dominic. "How long letter take, Thailand to America?" he asked.

Dominic shrugged. "One to two weeks, I think Mom said." He shot me a puzzled glance, then looked back at Bia.

I didn't blame Dominic for being puzzled. I was curious too. Why had Bia changed the subject? Didn't he even *know* what was in the letter? How could a person forget something as important as a self-description he had written to his new family? And why had that self-description been so inaccurate? His personality seemed just as different from the character of the letter as his appearance was from the photograph. For a moment, I didn't know what to say.

And then all at once I understood. Like the photo, showing him as a monk, the letter must have been an attempt to make a good impression on Mom and Dad. Maybe someone had even written it for him, which would explain the fluency of the letter, in contrast to his rocky spoken English. In that case, he could easily have forgotten some of the bogus details. And I, for one, was certainly glad that he *was* so different from the fanatically studious nerd he had led us to expect.

It was a good thing that Mom and Dad had missed this conversation. I stood up. "Come on, Bia," I said, rescuing him from Dominic. "If you want another cigarette, I'll go outside with you."

But Dominic got up too. "There's something else I've been wanting to ask you," he began. "Do you believe in spirits? Do you think—"

"Dominic," I said, giving him a look.

Dominic sighed. But he was basically a good kid, not a serious pest, and he stayed inside.

I was sure Bia would be glad to get away from Dominic's questions. But in the brief flare of his lighter I could see that his face was still guarded.

And then a bat whizzed overhead, and he flinched and spun around, almost dropping the lighter.

"Just a bat," I told him, surprised that someone as cool as Bia would be so startled by it. "They're attracted by the neighbors' pool."

"Bat?" he said, tossing the lighter casually in his palm, though his hand seemed to be shaking a little. "Your brother, Dominic. Know about Thai spirit. Really smart boy, huh?" he commented, his tone of voice more suspicious than complimentary.

"A brain. And it gets him into trouble sometimes."

"Trouble?" he said warily.

I wanted to lighten things up, so I gave him my Dominic spiel in simplified form, a humorous history of his exploits: At the age of two Dominic had effortlessly activated the fire alarm and sprinkler system at the newspaper where Dad worked, causing a tremendous uproar. He was only nine when he figured out how to make free long-distance calls by very precisely jiggling the buttons under the phone receiver a certain way—we had narrowly avoided getting into big trouble with the phone company. At ten, he had unleashed a devilish virus in the computer system at his elementary school. It had devoured the grade point averages of his entire class, and the principal had not been amused.

I was basically just making conversation. But, to my surprise, Bia seemed fascinated and impressed—especially by the story about the school computer system and its effect on grades and records.

"That true? Dominic, he really do *that?*" he asked.

"Why would I lie? I told you, he's a brain, a wizard. He can do anything."

"Wizard?"

I explained.

"Oh . . . *wizard,*" he said, his voice changing. "I see. Have wizard in Thailand."

"I didn't mean it *literally.*"

But he wasn't listening now. "Dominic wizard," Bia murmured, and took a last thoughtful pull on his current cigarette, staring past me. "Very good to know that. He say letter take one or two week from Thailand?"

"That's what he said. Why does it matter so much?"

"No matter. Just mean . . ." He didn't finish.

"It means what? What were you going to say?" I asked him.

"You like dancing, Julie?"

"Huh?"

"I really like. In Bangkok, big club, video, music, many light. All night, dancing." He paused, watching me. "Meet many girl," he added slyly.

"How can you go dancing all night if you have to study all the time?" I asked him.

"I really like," he said. "We go dancing, Julie?"

"Sure, I'd like to go dancing," I said. "But we—"

Another bat streaked by and he jumped again, as startled as the first time. "What's the matter?" I asked him. "Aren't there bats in—"

"Julie!" Mom called, stepping out onto the deck. "I need some help. And Bia, you must be exhausted after flying halfway around the world. Don't you want to get some sleep?"

He turned and walked slowly toward her. On the deck he *wai*ed her and said, "Yes. Really sleepy. Thank you."

Inside the house, Dominic said, "Bia, I wanted to ask you about the—"

"He's tired, Dominic," Mom said. "You'll have plenty of time for all your questions later."

But Bia, who had resisted Dominic's questions only a few minutes before, now seemed ready to answer him. "Yes? Please ask, Dominic."

"Do you have a spirit house, in Thailand?"

Bia's smile faded. "Spirit house," he murmured. His eyes flicked toward his reflection in the glass door again. Or was he looking out into the yard?

"Do you have a spirit house?" Dominic patiently repeated.

"Everybody have."

"Does your spirit house look like this one?" Dominic showed him a picture in his library book about Thailand, and we all looked. The miniature house stood on a pedestal in a garden. It seemed to be made out of stone and was very elaborately carved, with a steeply sloping roof.

"No," Bia said. "My spirit house more small, made of wood. One in photo for temple."

"Why are there flowers piled up in front of it? How does it work, anyway?" Dominic asked him.

"In Thailand, many spirit," Bia said reluctantly. "Everybody have spirit house, make nice, give flower. Bad spirit go there, stay out of big house."

"So that means that spirit houses *attract* bad spirits, right? What kind of bad spirits?"

Bia reached for the cigarettes in his shirt pocket, then glanced at Mom and instead put his hand to his neck, touching the delicate green pendant. "One spirit . . . called *Phii-Gaseu*," he said. His voice dropped slightly.

"What's it like?" Dominic pressed him, oblivious to Bia's hesitancy.

"Maybe he doesn't want to talk about it," I said.

"Is okay. If Dominic want to know," Bia said, and went on, rather grimly, his voice even quieter now. *"Phii-Gaseu* . . . look like lady head with . . . What the word? Oh, yes, like lady head with, uh, *entrail?"*

"Yes, go on, entrails, intestines, guts. What about them?" Dominic urged him.

Bia cleared his throat. "Look like lady head . . . lady head with no body and entrail coming from neck. Very bad spirit."

"Why does the bad spirit have to be a *woman?"* Mom predictably objected. "Aren't there—"

"Did you ever *see* one?" Dominic interrupted eagerly. "And aren't you worried that *we* don't have a spirit house? Doesn't that mean spirits might come around and bother us?"

"Don't think have Thai spirit in America," Bia said. But he glanced quickly out into the dark garden again. I remembered how startled he had been by the bats.

"Yes, but maybe they followed you here, because you're a Thai person," Dominic suggested. "And because there's no spirit house, maybe one of those ladies with intestines dangling out of her neck might start hanging around here. Don't you think it might be a good idea if we had our *own* spirit house?"

Bia firmly shook his head. "No. Not good idea. Forget it."

"Really?" Dominic said, disappointed. Then he thought of something else. "Bia, did *you* ever make a bargain with a spirit, ask it to do something for you? And if you did, did it actually come true? And did you—"

"Really sleepy now," Bia said abruptly. He *wai*ed Mom and Dad again, bowing more deeply this time, and strolled upstairs.

As soon as Bia was gone Mom asked me, "What were you talking about out there? Did he tell *you* anything about himself? He's such an appealing boy. But I wish he'd be a little less polite and a little more spontaneous."

I didn't want to tell her that he loved game shows and made a habit of staying out all night at clubs. "He didn't say much," I said.

"He seems worried about spirits," Dominic said.

"Oh, he was just embarrassed," Mom said. "He must know we don't have superstitions like that in this country."

"I still think he's worried about spirits," Dominic said. "And I know what to do about it."

3

Gloria phoned the next morning, Saturday, before Bia got up. "How's it going, Julie? Is the foreign student as bad as you thought? Are you okay?"

"Sure, I'm okay," I said. Of course I had complained to her and Lynette about the awful foreign student Mom was inflicting on me. But now I didn't know what to tell her. I was sure Gloria and Lynette would think Bia was gorgeous. When they met Bia they would probably go after him—they had no reason not to, since I was supposed to be going with Mark—and they were both very attractive and popular with boys. What if Bia liked them better than me?

"Tell me all about him, Julie. I'm your friend. I'm here to sympathize with you."

I was holding the phone slightly away from my ear—Gloria's voice carries. "Well, the foreign student got here. And now we're all really busy getting him settled in. So, I have to go now, Gloria. I'll call you later, okay?"

We usually didn't have a sit-down lunch together, but today, because of Bia, Mom decided we would all have sandwiches on the deck. Of course, I had to help her, and didn't want to, and she immediately started criticizing me for sulking and for being sloppy with the mayonnaise. "You should pay attention to Bia," she said. "*He's* very neat about everything he does."

Before I could scream at her Bia appeared and began unobtrusively helping us. Mom and I had to stop bickering.

And lunch was surprisingly pleasant. Bia told Dad how nice the yard was and asked him to name the various plants. He got them both talking about their jobs—Dad is a newspaper editor, Mom a professor of Women's Studies at the university. He asked Dominic about computers. In front of Bia I didn't grumble, and Mom refrained from criticizing my clothes and telling me I was wearing too much makeup. But I was sure we'd fall back into our normal patterns as soon as we got accustomed to his presence.

Still, I could see that Mom and Dad were relieved that Bia was turning out to be so nice. I realized now that they must have been a little apprehensive about what it would be like to have this stranger living with us. Now they could begin to relax.

They had gone to a great deal of trouble and expense to bring Bia over here. They hadn't arranged it through the usual foreign-exchange student agencies. Bia had been recommended to them by a visiting lecturer at the university who had taught in Thailand.

First they wrote to his family and his school, proposing to bring him over here for a year. After that they had to get his school records and present them to the principal of my high school. Then the principal had to fill out something called an I-20 form, which confirmed that

Thamrongsak would be accepted as a student. That had to be sent to the American embassy in Bangkok, along with a signed guarantee from Mom and Dad that they would be responsible for all his expenses while he was in this country. Supporting him for a year wasn't going to be cheap. And there were the immigration fees to be taken care of, and lots more lengthy forms to be filled out. They had even thought to send him a tourist guide to the city, so he'd know something about the place he'd be living in.

It all took a lot of time and expensive phone calls, and Mom and Dad had to keep sending over money for postage and other details, since Bia's family was so poor. They also had to buy him a round-trip ticket, which was complicated from this end and of course also cost a great deal.

After all that, it must have been very satisfying for Mom and Dad to see how pleasant Bia was, how polite. Today there wasn't even the usual discussion about doing the dishes when we finished eating. Bia automatically began carrying things in from the deck, and Dominic and I both wanted to help him.

Dominic had spent the morning in his basement workshop. When the lunch dishes were finished, Bia asked to see Dominic's computer, and the two of them went up to Dominic's third-floor room. I wondered about that; Bia had shown no interest in computers until *after* I had told him that Dominic could do almost anything with them. I also felt a little jealous, hearing them laughing up there.

At dinner on Saturday, Bia continued to answer Dominic's detailed questions about the architecture of spirit houses and other customs relating to spirits. The location of the spirit house was very important, it seemed. It was decided before the main house even went up, when they laid the foundation. They would make measurements at that stage, to find a place on the property where the shadow of the main house would never fall.

I wanted Dominic to lay off the spirit business. Bia didn't like talking about it. And Mom and Dad thought it was silly. For once I agreed with them. "I really like your pendant, Bia," I said. "I've never seen anything like it."

He smiled at me in a way that seemed genuine, not studied. Was he relieved to get away from the subject of spirits? "Thank you. Real jade Buddha. Make good luck."

"It looks very expensive," Mom said. "I must admit, I was kind of surprised to see you wearing something that seems so valuable. I mean, when your family is so . . ." Mom wasn't quite tactless enough to say in so many words that his family was poor. But Bia got the message. His face went blank again.

"Maybe it's an heirloom, or a gift," I said.

"Yes," Bia said, nodding at me. "Gift from my good friend, Chai."

And later on, in the backyard, he thanked me again for helping him with my family. "You are really good friend, Julie," he said quietly. "I am not forget."

We ate breakfast late on Sunday, after waiting for Bia to get up—he was still adjusting to the twelve-hour time change. Then Dominic disappeared. It wasn't long before Bia asked me where he was.

"He's probably down in his workshop in the basement," I said. "That's where he builds his gadgets. He started some new project yesterday."

"Yesterday Saturday," Bia murmured, his face serious. "Saturday very bad day start some thing."

"Why? What difference does it make?"

"Because, Saturday, it mean . . ." Then he shook his head, lifting his hand, as if it were too difficult to explain. "Maybe I go down. Say hello."

"Well, he usually doesn't like people bothering him down there—it's kind of his private place," I told him. "The door's probably locked. Why don't we go for a walk?"

"Walk?" he said doubtfully.

"Well, you haven't seen anything of the neighborhood yet. We won't go very far."

We didn't. Bia walked slowly, smoked continuously, and got out of breath on the slightest incline. I was surprised at how out of shape he was, when he seemed so well put together.

"Do you think you're going to like it here?" I asked him.

"Not matter if like," he said, looking straight ahead. "Matter for future."

"Why is coming here so important for your future?"

"Study at American school. Learn English good. Make big, big difference in Thailand."

"What kind of difference?"

"Better job. Maybe guide with tourist, or working at hotel. Need education, English, for good job like that."

"But since you're such a good student, couldn't you get a scholarship to college in Thailand, without having to come over here?" I asked him. "Especially after what your teachers said about you."

He didn't seem to have heard me.

"Didn't they tell you what they said?" I asked him. "Your teachers gave you the highest recommendations. They said you were unusually brilliant."

"Many, many good student. Very, very few place in school, very small money for many student. That is life." He shrugged, his mouth a hard line. And he wouldn't say any more about it.

If he'd looked the way he had in the photo, I wouldn't have cared that he was so elusive; I would have assumed he was just shy and awkward and cautious about this new situation. But he wasn't shy or awkward; he was smooth and cool and extraordinarily handsome. And I was very curious about the mystery he presented.

Why had he forgotten about the photograph and the letter? Why didn't he know what his teachers had said about him? And why, every once in a while, did he seem to be covering up a kind of nervousness? Was he really afraid of spirits, as Dominic believed?

Or was he worried about something else?

4

Bia was asleep when Mom and Dad left for work on Monday. As Dominic and I cleaned up the breakfast dishes, I thought about how I could get Bia to open up about himself. I hoped Dominic wouldn't be hanging around us all day.

Dominic put down the last pot and looked at his watch. "I wonder when he's going to get up," he said. "I need to get more data from him, about spirits and things."

"Oh, that spirit stuff," I said. I knew Bia didn't like talking about spirits. I couldn't blame him for wanting to adopt an American point of view as quickly as he could. "Maybe you shouldn't keep bugging him about spirits so much," I said.

"But it's the most interesting stuff he's said about Thailand!" Dominic protested.

"Yeah, but you don't understand, Dominic. It's not good to encourage him to talk about it. He wants to be like American kids, to fit in. If people at school get the idea he believes in spirits, they'll think he's weird."

"Conformist!" Dominic accused me, with a look of scorn. "Anyway, your friends won't know if he talks to *me* about spirits."

In a way, I knew Dominic's attitude was better than mine, that learning about a foreign culture should have been more important to me than peer pressure. But it wasn't. I was glad that Bia wanted to come across cool. And I didn't doubt that he would, despite his fractured English. "Just don't bug him," I said. "Give him some time to adjust."

Dominic sighed. "All right, I won't bug him," he said. "I don't have time to hang around waiting for him all day anyway. I have all this work to do on my new project. I want to finish it before school starts."

"What *is* this new project?" I asked him.

"Oh, nothing," he said, on his way out of the room. He was in his basement workshop with the door closed, absorbed in whatever it was he was building, when Bia finally came downstairs around ten.

At the bottom of the stairs Bia said, in a hushed voice, "Your parent? At work?" He looked rakish and a little tough today, in black jeans and a black T-shirt with the words "Rome Club" scrawled across it in large white letters. Many of his shirts, I was noticing, had slogans or logos on them.

"They won't be home until six. You want some breakfast?"

"Don't trouble. I make."

I followed him into the kitchen. He already knew where everything was. Without a wasted movement he very calmly and efficiently put water on to boil, squeezed an orange, and heated up a cup of coffee in the microwave. He put two eggs in a saucepan, poured boiling water over them, and then immediately poured the water out and cracked the eggs into a mug. They were still completely raw and must have been barely warm, but he spooned them into his mouth with gusto.

"You look as if you make your own breakfast every day of your life," I commented.

"I do," he said, and swallowed the last spoonful of egg.

"You mean your mother's at work or something?"

He put down the spoon and looked at me for a moment, as if considering something. "Don't live with parent," he finally said. "Have room in Bangkok."

This was unexpected—and very intriguing. "You have your own place?"

"Share with friend. Leave school. Must work in Bangkok. Send money to parent, not live off parent. Have room for more than one year. Much better, live there."

"But I thought you were in school," I said, confused. "Your principal, your teachers, they sent us these forms and things."

"They remember me, like me. Think special boy. They really happy your parent give me opportunity come here and study."

"Oh. I see." It was strange that no one had told us he had been out of school, working, for a year.

But so what if he had dropped out? The fact that he was too poor to go to school in Thailand only made him *more* deserving of the chance to come here. And I couldn't help being impressed that he had his own place. That must be why he seemed sophisticated, older, even though he looked the same age as me.

He leaned forward abruptly, his elbows on the table. "Please, Julie. Don't tell parent leave school, work, have room. Okay?"

Telling me he had his own place was the first glimpse he had given me of his real life, and now he seemed to be regretting it, worried that he had said too much. "I won't tell them," I quickly assured him. "But . . . why don't you want them to know?"

He looked down at the table, running his hand over the spoon. "Don't want them think I lie. Don't want them think not serious student boy." He looked up at me again. "Okay, Julie?"

Had he purposely neglected to tell them that information? I didn't really understand why he might have done that. But this was what I had been hoping for. He was beginning to trust me, to let me in on things he seemed to be hiding from the others. "Of course I won't tell them, Bia. You can trust me. I promise."

"Thank you, Julie. You really good friend," he said, gazing at me with serious, steady alertness, as though I were a painting in a museum. But there was unexpected warmth in his voice when he said softly, "Really important have good friend in America. Am not forget."

He sounded so sincere that I almost felt a little guilty. He seemed to think I was doing him this tremendous favor, when I was really just trying to satisfy my curiosity. "So how did you support yourself? What was your job, anyway?" I asked him after a brief silence; the directness of his stare was a little unsettling.

He looked around. "Dominic? Where he go?"

"Oh, he's down in the basement, working on his project. He'll probably be there all day. Don't worry, he won't bother us."

"Project? What is project? Same he start on unlucky day, Saturday?"

"*I* don't know. Some secret thing. He wouldn't tell me. I'm sure it isn't very interesting."

"What isn't very interesting?" Dominic said, walking into the kitchen.

Bia smiled. "I am sure Julie is wrong and your project is *very* interesting, Wizard Dominic. I can see?"

"Oh, no," Dominic said instantly. "It's not ready yet. Don't go down there. Really. It's . . . a secret, a surprise."

"Project," Bia said, not willing to drop the subject. "Is project you start on Saturday?"

"Saturday?" Dominic shrugged. "Yeah, I guess I did. So what?"

"Saturday very, *very* unlucky day, start to make some thing," Bia said, his voice suddenly serious. "Hope nothing important."

"Saturday is an unlucky day to start building things?" Dominic said curiously, coming closer.

I was irritated with both of them—with Bia for asking Dominic about his stupid project, and with Dominic for encouraging Bia to talk about these silly superstitions. I was going to have to make it clear to Bia that the kids at school would get the wrong idea about him if he talked to *them* this way. "Hey, listen, Dominic," I started to say. "Why don't you—"

But Bia interrupted me. "Sunday, Tuesday, unlucky day start to make thing. But Saturday *most* unlucky day of all. Everybody know."

"Saturday is an unlucky day to start making what *kind* of thing?" Dominic asked him, looking worried.

"House," Bia said, with conviction. "Never, *never* start to make house on Saturday."

"But . . . but what would happen if you did?" Dominic said, swallowing, sounding a little sick. I couldn't believe he was actually taking this stuff seriously.

"Start to make house on Saturday, bring trouble, bring great misfortune to owner of house." Bia looked at me. "You don't know this? You don't know what day they start to make *this* house?"

I sighed. "Of *course* not! Come on. Nobody pays attention to stuff like that in America. And they'll just think you're nuts if you go around talking about it."

"But Bia, what if a person didn't *know?*" Dominic said urgently. "Wouldn't it be okay then?"

But finally Bia seemed to be catching on. "Please, don't be so worry, Dominic. Julie right. Different here. Is custom for Thai house, not America house. Here, no problem. In Thai, *mai pen rai,* mean 'never mind.' And you don't build house, so don't need worry. Okay?"

But Dominic didn't seem particularly relieved. "Yeah, well, I *hope* it's different here," he said grimly. He paused for a moment, thinking. "And anyway, it *wasn't* Saturday in Thailand when I started it. It's twelve hours later there. So that would count as Sunday. And you said that's not as bad as Saturday. Right?" he pressed Bia, with a kind of tense eagerness.

"Dominic, what's the matter with you? What are you so scared of?" Despite my impatience with this topic, Dominic's reaction made me curious. Though his projects frequently did backfire, he usually never worried about that possibility until it actually happened. "What is this thing you're building, anyway?"

"Nothing. A surprise," Dominic said, closing up. He turned and wandered back to the basement.

"Now listen, Bia," I said. "I hope you're not going to

talk about things like that, spirits and lucky and unlucky days, to the kids at school. I mean, it's different with Dominic. He's weird—and anyway, it doesn't matter what he thinks. But the other kids, my friends, they might think it's a little, I don't know, peculiar." I was trying to put it as tactfully as possible. "I mean, I'm not putting down your customs or anything. I know it's different in Thailand. I just want the other kids to like you, that's all."

He was looking at me in that steady way again. "I think you care about me little bit, Julie. Help me not to make mistake in America. Thank you very much."

Bia and I spent a lot of time together the week before school started, with Mom and Dad at work all day, and Dominic preoccupied in the basement. I didn't get to know him as well as I would an American boy. But he did begin to relax with me, to smile more than he did when other people were around. We didn't talk every minute we were together. Sometimes, watching me, he would hum, in a sweet, husky voice, snatches of tunes that he told me were popular songs in Thailand. I liked it when he did that, though it made me a little self-conscious. I wondered what the songs were about, and what he was thinking about me.

I never called Gloria back as I'd told her I would on Saturday. She called one more time, concerned about how I was doing, and Lynette called too. I assured them I was okay, just very busy with my family, and I'd tell them all about it at school. They were my friends; they were curious, of course, but not offended. And with Bia around, it was easy to put them out of my mind.

On Wednesday the whole family went out to dinner downtown, and we showed Bia some of the sights. As

31

always, he was very polite but said very little—until we drove past the colored fountain at City Hall Plaza. He was clearly impressed by the changing patterns of illuminated water. He leaned out the window to stare back at it, then said, "Never see thing like that before. Nobody tell me they make water like firework in America!"

"But Bia," Mom said, turning to look at him from the front seat, "that exact same fountain was on the cover of the guidebook we sent you."

"Guidebook," he said, his face suddenly expressionless.

"Even if you didn't bother reading the book, you must have noticed that fountain on the cover," Mom said, sounding a little hurt. "I was surprised that you never thanked us for it. And we thought it was such a nice gift."

Bia didn't say anything. And I realized what had probably happened. We had sent the book to his parents' house, of course—I had mailed it myself—and they must have forgotten to give it to him. I was about to explain that it was his parents' fault Bia hadn't mentioned the book—and then remembered that nobody was supposed to know Bia didn't live at home. "Oh, no!" I said, slapping my forehead.

"*Now* what, Julie?" Mom said.

"I . . . I forgot to mail the guidebook. I was doing a lot of errands that day. I must have just put it down someplace and left it there. I don't remember ever taking it to the post office."

Mom groaned. "Oh, Julie, when are you going to grow up? How could you be so irresponsible?" But that was all she said. She was still being artificially polite in front of Bia; otherwise she would have berated me about it all the way home.

I didn't mind taking the blame. Bia, sitting next to me in the dark backseat, squeezed my hand, and then held it for a long moment.

The next morning, when Mom and Dad were gone and Dominic was down in the basement, Bia found me in my room, where I was getting some stuff ready for school. "I come in?" he said from the doorway.

I turned around from the desk. "Sure."

He walked toward me, smiling, holding the jade Buddha pendant in front of him with both hands. "For you, Julie," he said. "For my special friend."

"Bia . . ." I started to protest.

But before I could say any more he had fastened the heavy gold chain around my neck. "For helping me with parent. Not telling secret. Make mother angry with you, to help me."

"But Bia, your pendant!" I said, looking down at it, feeling strangely close to tears. "How can you give this away? It's so important to you. And you said it brought you good luck."

"Now don't need good luck. Have special friend who help me. I am never forget. And hope . . ." He paused, watching me. "And hope you never forget too," he said slowly, holding me with his eyes. He touched me briefly on the cheek with one hand, then turned and silently left the room.

And now I was blinking back tears. I had never been so moved by a gift before. Nothing anybody else had given me could mean as much as this precious pendant from a poor boy like Bia. It was probably the most valuable thing he had ever had in his life. He wouldn't have given it to me if he didn't really like me.

With two fingers, I lifted the delicately carved jade

Buddha up to my face to get a better look at it, stretching out the chain. The clasp that held the heavy chain around my neck came open unexpectedly and the Buddha slipped out of my hand to the floor. I picked it up quickly, glad that Bia hadn't seen me drop it. As I carefully refastened the chain I promised myself that I would get the clasp fixed right away.

I couldn't wait to see what Gloria and Lynette would think when they got their eyes on Bia and then saw the beautiful piece of jewelry he had given me. Now they could meet him. It would be clear to everybody that this handsome and worldly boy was very attached to me.

And then I remembered Mark. I knew he was returning this week; he might phone me at any time. What would I say when he did? I was going to have to deal with him soon. He seemed sort of boring and ordinary to me now, compared to Bia. No American boy had Bia's mystery and intrigue. But was I really ready to break up with Mark because of Bia? I didn't want to think about it.

I pushed Mark from my mind. What mattered was that Bia trusted me now. I still didn't understand him too well, but after today he might share more about himself with me. He had been so unreachable at first that it was especially gratifying to have finally won him over. That made me very happy—and also rather pleased with myself.

But on Friday everything changed.

5

"My project is finished," Dominic announced when Mom and Dad came home from work on Friday evening. "I want everybody to come and see it." But he didn't seem proud or enthusiastic, as he usually was at such moments. He seemed nervous, even a little scared. "Come on out in back," Dominic said, and glanced apprehensively at Bia.

Bia gave one of his rare smiles. "Ah, secret project. Want to see very much."

We saw it as soon as we stepped out onto the deck— a little dark wooden structure standing on a platform supported by two-by-fours, about four feet off the ground, near the back end of the yard.

The light was fading, and I could not make out the details of the little building from this distance. But the only thing it could be was a spirit house. We all stopped and looked at Bia.

He stared at it for a long moment, as his smile melted away. Then he turned to Dominic, his lips parted, not speaking.

"For you, Bia," Dominic said solemnly. "A spirit house, to make you feel at home."

Bia said nothing.

"Is something wrong?" Dominic asked him, more worried now. "Come and look at it. Tell me if it's okay. Be honest. I can change it, fix it. Come on."

We moved slowly toward it through the darkening yard. "Well, that was very thoughtful of you, Dominic," Dad said, to break the uneasy silence. But I seemed to remember Bia firmly telling Dominic that he *didn't* want a spirit house here. And the closer we got to the thing, the less I liked it.

There was something ugly, even a little forbidding, about the design and the dimensions of the small building. The roof was steeply slanted, with curved, pointed wooden ornaments along the peak and poking up at the eaves. There was a little flight of steps going up from the platform to a porch at the front, which had a railing with diamond-shaped supports. A square doorway was cut in the front wall of the house, through which I could see the empty darkness within. And somehow I wished the roof were not quite so steep, the building a little less narrow, and that it had been brightly colored instead of stained a dull dark brown.

We stopped a foot away from it, Bia still silent, Dominic watching him with painful intensity. And my heart went out to Dominic. Though the building was somewhat rough and primitive, he had put a great deal of work into the thing, with all its ornamental carving. He had even thought to place a rose blossom from Mom's garden on the porch, carefully positioned exactly in the center.

And then Bia *wai*ed the spirit house, holding his head

bowed and his fingertips almost touching his forehead for longer than he had ever done to Mom and Dad.

When Bia finally lifted his head, Dominic burst out, "Well? Say something, Bia! Is it okay? Do you like it?"

"Thank you, Dominic," Bia said, not smiling. "I know you work very hard to make this."

Bia was clearly unhappy. Dominic knew it and was disappointed. "I wanted to make it as much as I could like the one in the book," he said, trying to cajole more of a response from Bia. "And the shadow of the house will never fall here—I checked and rechecked my measurements, I was extra careful about that."

"You did a very good job, Dominic," Mom said.

"Couldn't have done it half as well myself," said Dad.

"It's really something, Dominic," I told him.

"Well, Bia, will it work?" Dominic begged him. "Will it attract the evil spirits, and protect you from them?"

Bia stared glumly at the dark little building. "Don't know, in America," he said, and I was almost angry at him for not at least *faking* an enthusiastic response, after all Dominic's hard work.

The phone rang. It was not loud, from out in the yard, but it startled Bia. His shoulders twitched as though someone had unexpectedly touched him on the back of the neck. Mom ran to get it.

Bia turned to Dominic and said, so softly it was barely audible, "Is true . . . you start to make spirit house on Saturday?"

"Well, yes," Dominic admitted. "But that can't really mean it will bring . . ." His voice faded unhappily.

"It's for you, Bia, from Thailand!" Mom called, hurrying toward us across the lawn.

"For me?" Bia said. The color drained from his face.

He put one hand to his throat, as if feeling for his pendant. But of course I was wearing the pendant now, and he slowly moved his head to look at me, his expression unreadable. It was hardly the reaction I would have expected to a call from home.

"For *you*," Mom said. "Don't just stand there. Go answer it. You *know* how much it costs from over there."

We watched Bia moving reluctantly toward the house, his hair lifted by the breeze, his black shirt fluttering.

"I'm sure he really likes the spirit house, Dom," Dad said, putting his hand on Dominic's shoulder. "It's probably a very serious religious object to him. That's why he was so subdued."

But Mom didn't seem interested in the spirit house now. "Funny," she said, still staring after Bia. "You'd think someone who cared about him enough to call him all the way from Thailand would know his nickname."

"What do you mean?" I asked her.

"The man on the phone wanted to speak to Thamrongsak. And I said yes, Bia was outside, I'd get him. And the guy said no, not a person named Bia. Thamrongsak."

6

When we went back inside Bia was off the phone; he must have gone up to his room. I started upstairs, hoping to have a few minutes alone with him. I was curious about the phone call, and his strange reaction to the spirit house. I wanted to ask him to be a little more enthusiastic about it, for Dominic's sake.

"Where are you going, Julie?" Mom barked at me. "You're supposed to be making supper."

"I'm starving," Dad said. "Aren't we ready to eat yet?"

We weren't. I trudged back down the stairs. I was starting to pull the fish out from under the broiler and Mom was unloading the dishwasher when the phone rang again. "Yes, she's here," Mom said, thrusting the receiver at me as I pushed the fish back into the oven. "And don't talk very long," she whispered. "Supper's already late."

"Hi, stranger," Gloria said.

"Oh, Gloria," I said. "Sorry I never called you back. We've just been so busy, with the foreign student and everything."

"Uh-huh," Gloria said. "Well, Julie, guess who's home? Mark. And guess who he called? Lynette. She just called to tell me. He's on his way to her house right now."

I didn't know what to say. I had thought I didn't care about Mark anymore, but now I felt a jealous pang. I was the one he'd been going out with before he left for Europe. I was the one he'd been writing to—I knew he hadn't sent Lynette or Gloria a single postcard. It was odd that he had instantly called Lynette, without even trying me first.

"Uh-huh," Gloria said knowingly. "I thought you'd be interested. Well, I guess you'll just have to cry on what's-his-name's shoulder."

I was stung by her tone. I'd thought she was my friend. Why was she being so nasty? "I really have to go," I said. "I'm late with supper."

I set the receiver down slowly, with a painful feeling of foreboding. I had worried about Mark's return, wondering what it would mean in relation to me and Bia. But Mark didn't know that. So why hadn't he called me? I was hurt and mystified. Did this mean Mark had dropped me? But why? I couldn't think of any reason for it.

Apparently Lynette hadn't hesitated an instant to agree to see him. And why had Gloria been so spiteful, rather than sympathetic about it? There were many times in the past when I hadn't called either of them for a few days; they had never been angry about it before. And being occupied with the foreign student was a logical explanation. But now, suddenly, the girl friends it had taken me so long to make last year seemed to have turned against me. And without Mark to give me status, would I be treated like the out-of-it new girl all over again?

But I had Bia, didn't I? He might not be one of the class leaders, like Mark was. But he cared about me. I was wearing his pendant. No one would see me as pathetic as long as I was with Bia. The girls would be impressed by his looks, and everybody would think he was cool—he knew how to make people like him. My status would hardly be diminished at all. I brightened a little.

When supper was ready I hurried up to get him. I knocked on his door, then stepped inside his room without waiting for an answer.

He was getting hastily to his feet, brushing off his pants, as though he had been kneeling on the floor. "Oh. Did I interrupt you?" I asked him.

"Yes," he said, not looking at me.

I was taken aback; it wasn't like him to be so rudely direct. "Well I just wanted to tell you it's time for supper." I smiled at him. "And also . . . thank you again for the pendant, Bia. I love wearing it. Nobody ever gave me anything as nice. It means—"

"Hungry now," he interrupted me, and walked toward the door.

"Bia!" I said. "What . . ."

He turned back from the doorway. "Supper," he said coolly. "You boring me." And he walked out of the room.

It was just as though he had slapped me in the face.

The meal began in silence. I'd been cooking pretty decently all week, but tonight the fish was burned, the mashed potatoes like glue. Dominic was more depressed than I'd ever seen him, moping over Bia's reaction to his spirit house. Dad, who doted on Dominic, seemed a little down on Bia too—and he gave me a nasty look when he tasted the fish, which wasn't like him. That hurt, and so did Gloria's spitefulness, and the fact that Mark had ignored me and rushed immediately to Lynette.

And what was the matter with Bia? Yes, he had always been somewhat distant. But yesterday he had given me the pendant and told me how special I was. And now he was worse than cool to me, he was insulting.

It was very strange how the world had changed so abruptly. There was something unnatural about the suddenness of it, something that gnawed at the corner of my mind but didn't surface.

Mom couldn't control her curiosity about Bia's phone call. "I hope you had good news from home," she started out, breaking the silence, not saying anything—at first—about the odd fact that the caller had not known Thamrongsak's familiar name.

"Everybody fine," Bia said.

"Was that your father who called?" Mom wanted to know.

He didn't confirm or deny it. "Family fine," he said again. "Food good tonight." He pushed mashed potatoes—which he hated—into his mouth.

It was obvious that he considered the phone call his own private business, which it was, and didn't want to talk about it. But Mom refused to drop the subject. And I wanted some answers too. If he would at least admit that he had had some bad news, that might explain his sudden change in attitude toward me. Maybe it was something he didn't want Mom and Dad to know, and he would tell me about it later, when we were alone.

"But if it was your father, then why didn't he know your familiar name?" Mom persisted.

"What you mean?" Bia asked.

"He didn't know the name Bia. Just Thamrongsak," Mom said, watching him.

He slowly chewed a mouthful of potato and swallowed it. "Neighbor make call to America, for father. Know English, little bit. Not know my nickname Bia."

Finally Mom gave up. But she was dissatisfied, irritable.

"How long take letter, Thailand to America?" Bia asked her.

"One or two weeks. Why?"

Bia shrugged and looked down at his plate.

"Well, Julie, you really outdid yourself tonight," Mom snapped at me. Bia's presence wasn't stopping her now. "This is barely edible. Did you think about how much this fish cost when you so casually let it burn?"

"It wasn't my fault. It was because Gloria called me up."

"It's never your fault, is it."

I managed to restrain myself from throwing down my fork and rushing upstairs. I wanted to be down there when supper was over so I could talk with Bia when he went out in the backyard to smoke.

But Bia stayed away from the backyard. He went out to the front of the house to smoke, on the street. I followed him out there anyway. And he still refused to say anything about the phone call, to admit he had heard any bad news. He did ask me if I thought my parents would call Thailand. "Call who?" I asked him. "Your family? Anyway, what reason do they have to call?" But he wouldn't say and did not seem reassured.

After that, he spent most of the weekend with Dominic, upstairs, at Dominic's computer. Not once did he go into the backyard, where we had had so many private talks.

I couldn't pretend that he wasn't avoiding me; I couldn't sleep on Friday or Saturday night, worrying about it. Was he angry because I had walked into his room without knocking on Friday evening, when he might have been praying? It seemed like an extreme reaction from someone who was usually so polite. But I didn't understand Thai customs; maybe interrupting someone at prayer was a terrible offense. His mysterious nature made it very difficult to guess what might be going on in his head. Dealing with an ordinary American boy would have been simple in comparison.

Dominic didn't stay quite as gloomy as he had been on Friday night. Bia had been upset by the spirit house, but he was certainly spending a lot of time with Dominic now, and that must have cheered him a little. Then, on Sunday night, Dominic asked me if Bia had said anything to me about the spirit house.

"He hardly talks to me at all," I told him. "Didn't you notice?"

But of course Dominic wasn't concerned about Bia's attitude toward me. "I wish he'd say *something*," Dominic said, sighing. "I keep putting fresh flowers in it, but he never even goes near it. I didn't mean to upset him. I wish I'd never built it."

"Then take it down, if you're so worried about it," I said, wishing my problems could be solved as easily.

"Oh, no!" Dominic said, sounding horrified. "That might make it even *worse!*"

"Well just forget about it then," I told him. "At least Bia's talking to you. What are you two working on upstairs, anyway?"

"I'm just helping him learn to write on the computer," Dominic said. "And playing math games with him. Funny how little math he knows. . . ."

Unlike Dominic, Dad hadn't forgiven Bia for his reaction to the spirit house. He was definitely colder to him. And though Mom could never be as obnoxious to anyone as she was to me, she was no longer on her best behavior with Bia.

On Sunday evening at supper she had the gall to criticize his English. He had answered a question of Dominic's by saying that in Thailand they rarely ate with "chopstick," and Mom said, "Didn't they teach you about plural nouns in your English classes?"

"Plural?" Bia said blankly.

"She means—" I started to say.

"I was just looking over your school records again. They show you got all A's in advanced conversational English," Mom interrupted me. "You'd think advanced English would have included something as basic as the plural noun."

It was a logical question, though I still felt like kicking her for putting him on the spot. But now that he understood, Bia had an answer. "Advance English in Thailand, not same as advance English in America," he said. "You hear other Thai student in advance English, you see."

"Hmph," Mom said, unconvinced.

After supper on Sunday, my last chance to talk with Bia before school started, he went right up to his room and stayed there. I lay awake all night. And then it was Monday morning, and I was more nervous than I had been on the first day of school last year, when I was new.

I slouched into the bathroom, feeling exhausted. I stared at my sallow, bleary-eyed reflection in the mirror. The first thing I saw was a pimple in the middle of my chin. Then I couldn't get my hair to fall right; my eyes were bloodshot, with dark circles around them. I had never looked worse in my life.

Not that my appearance mattered anymore. Mark had already dropped me for Lynette. Gloria had suddenly become openly hostile to me. Bia wouldn't look at me or talk to me.

He hardly said a word on the walk to school. I wanted to know why he was angry, why he had stopped caring about me. But it was clear that asking him would be pointless. He behaved as though I weren't there, not looking at me, keeping well away from me on the sidewalk. There was no way anyone would get the idea that he liked me, even though he had given me the pendant.

I steeled myself as we neared the school. Hordes of kids were gathering on the front steps. I spotted Gloria and Lynette and Mark at the edge of the crowd. Mark had his arm around Lynette's shoulder. They had seen us now. They didn't wave or smile, they just watched us approaching. I concentrated on putting one foot in front of the other. I had never felt so pathetic in my life.

And all day it got worse.

7

Mark, Gloria, and Lynette greeted me with a kind of cool smugness, though Mark did seem a little embarrassed too. As soon as I introduced Bia they forgot about me. In less than a minute Gloria was actively flirting and Lynette was being as friendly as she could get away with in front of Mark. Occasionally Gloria and Lynette managed to drag their eyes away from Bia long enough to cast looks of approval and awed amazement at each other. No one was impressed by the pendant on my neck; no one even noticed it.

And I had worried, before Bia arrived, that a nerdy foreign student would hurt my status! Already, on the first day of school, smooth, cool Bia was the focus of interest, and I was the outcast.

"Come on, Bia, time to meet the principal." My voice sounded as warped and fuzzy to my ears as an old record. I started edging him away, up the steps.

"Bia, try to get into Rothschild's English class," Lynette called after him.

"No, Rothschild's a bore, take *Becker's* class," Gloria brayed.

"No, no, Becker hates men. Take Rothschild," Lynette insisted.

"Ignore her! She's lying. The name is Becker!" Gloria shouted.

Bia kept turning back to smile at them as I urged him toward the doors. "You have nice friend, Julie. Really pretty girl. Like very much."

"Great," I muttered. "I'm so happy to hear it. Now you better use some of your charm on the principal. This way."

The school secretary let Mrs. Keating know we were there and then told us to go right in. When we entered her office Mrs. Keating was already striding from behind her desk, her hand extended, smiling at Bia. And then Bia *wai*ed her.

I glanced quickly through the open door, but no one in the outer office had noticed. Bia's head was still bowed when I turned back. Mrs. Keating didn't seem to know what to do.

"It's . . . a sign of respect," I said, blushing.

"A welcome change from what I get from most students," Mrs. Keating said, her smile returning. She actually seemed interested as she asked the usual questions about his trip, and what he thought of it here, and Bia told her that America was very beautiful, and very strange. I could see that she liked.him already.

"Your teacher recommendations and test scores are extremely impressive, especially in math and English," she said, speaking very fast, as always. "Otherwise, we couldn't have accepted you, of course, since we have no facilities for ESL students here. But judging from your marks in English, and your writing sample, you shouldn't be at even a minimal disadvantage due to low comprehension."

Bia nodded, wisely not saying anything. I knew he had no idea what she was talking about.

Mrs. Keating's smile faded a bit. "Your English *is* at an acceptable level of fluency, isn't it?" she asked him.

"Oh, his English is *fine*," I said quickly, before she had a chance to catch on that it wasn't. "Except, sometimes when people talk really fast he misses things. So it might make sense to put him in some of my classes."

It had struck me, watching Bia and Mrs. Keating, that he wouldn't have a clue about what was going on in any of his classes. Without a lot of help he would be lost. I understood how important this year was to his future. He'd been unfriendly to me for a few days, but I really didn't want him to fail in school and lose his chance for a better life. And if I helped him, his attitude might change back—he might forgive me for whatever it was I had done to offend him.

"You want to be in some classes together?" Mrs. Keating said. "Well, you'll have to check with Mr. Fowler about your schedules—he's Bia's homeroom teacher. Better hurry, you've only got a few minutes. It's very nice to meet you, Bia, and I'm sure you'll have a wonderful year with us."

"Thank you. I think I really like school here," he told her. "Not like Thailand. School principal there always much older than student." She was beaming at him as we left the office.

"Do you want me in some of your classes?" I asked him, out in the hallway. "I might be able to help you a little."

"Thank you," he said, eyeing a pair of senior girls.

There were kids in Mr. Fowler's room already, some of whom I knew. I was aware of their eyes on us as we approached the desk. I realized, too late, that I had forgotten to tell Bia not to *wai* Mr. Fowler. And when he did *wai* him I glanced quickly over at the others. Most of them hadn't noticed. Those who had seemed more curious than contemptuous.

I did most of the talking, explaining that Mrs. Keating had said Mr. Fowler might be able to get Bia into some of my classes. Of course Fowler had to object that it was rather late to be rearranging Bia's schedule and wanted to know why he hadn't been told earlier, as though it were my fault. But I didn't back down. It was very clear to me that Bia wouldn't make it on his own; he'd flunk out of school in a matter of weeks without me there to help him. I also wanted to be in his classes so I could keep my eye on him for purely selfish reasons. I didn't like the way Gloria and Lynette had already tried to appropriate him.

There was no way to get him into my American history or math classes. Still, Bia was very clever about figuring out how to coordinate three of our other classes. Fowler noticed that. He also noticed how courteous Bia was about the whole thing, and how Bia made sure to express his gratitude to him for helping us out.

"Of course, this is all just on paper," Fowler told Bia. "You're still going to have to confirm it with the individual teachers. Although, now that I've met you, I don't think any teacher would object to having you as a student."

The bell rang.

"See you second period, Bia," I said.

He met my eyes briefly. And on his face was a searching expression I had never seen before. I caught a flash of uncertainty in the way his lips were slightly parted. He was unsure about being here on his own, with all these strangers speaking a foreign language.

He *wasn't* cool to the core; he had a vulnerable side too—and he had just allowed me to see it. I couldn't help being touched.

And then Fowler, looking harried, was directing Bia to a desk. I hurried to homeroom.

I didn't hear a word Campbell said in first period; I stared into space, worrying about Bia. I kept trying to tell myself that he was used to being on his own, that he knew very well how to deal with people, and that his transcript from Thailand proved he was a much better student than I was. But I still worried.

Because now I was beginning to suspect that his transcript had been tampered with somehow, a clever fake. It was obvious to me that he couldn't have passed an advanced English test. And Dominic had said he didn't know much math. So where had those brilliant scores come from? Had he falsified his school records in Thailand? What other explanation was there for the discrepancy?

Maybe he hadn't merely faked the records—maybe he had just faked everything else.

I thought of the photograph. Bia really *didn't* look much like the boy who had originally written to us. His inadequate English, his personality and interests were completely different from what the letter had indicated. And today I had seen that, even handicapped by his limited English, he was a talented actor who could use his charm to make whatever impression he wanted on people. Had he substituted himself for the other boy? Was that why he had been so worried by the phone call from Thailand? Had something gone wrong with his scheme?

I tried to concentrate on what Campbell was saying. But I couldn't stop thinking about Bia, and I couldn't convince myself that I was imagining things. All the evidence could easily indicate that Bia was pretending to be somebody he wasn't. And that possibility led directly to the most unpleasant question of all.

If Bia was an impostor, then what had happened to the *real* Thamrongsak Tan-ngarmtrong?

"Julie? Earth to Julie," Campbell said. He must have asked me a question. The whole class was laughing at me.

It was a terrible day, worse than the first day of school last year. The teachers were brusque and un-friendly to me. I felt exhausted in gym class and was clumsier than usual. Afterward, in the dressing room, I noticed a second ugly pimple on my chin. My hair was lank and greasy, though I had just washed it. Gloria and Lynette looked better than I had ever seen them, full of bounce and energy, flirting happily with Bia. And he flirted back.

All I could think about during last period was what I would say to him after school. But he was out of his seat as soon as the bell rang, as if he were trying to get away from me. I rushed after him, ignoring what the other kids might think, and touched his arm as he was on his way out the door.

"What?" he said, poised and distant, no hint of vulnerability now.

"I need to talk to you."

"Not now," he said. "Have date with Gloria." He hurried away.

I walked home alone, still thinking compulsively about him.

It was obvious that Bia had been taking advantage of me—as he took advantage of everybody and everything that came his way—to get whatever it was he wanted. He had lied easily to Mom and Dad—and then given me the pendant so that I would keep lying to them too. As soon as he had found out that Dominic could alter school records with computers, he had gone out of his way to be nice to him, to answer his questions—and to learn from him about computers. Today I had seen him charm Mrs. Keating so she wouldn't notice what his English was really like. He did all these things with the most natural aplomb. But that wasn't even the worst of it.

It seemed very likely to me now that he wasn't Thamrongsak Tan-ngarmtrong. I remembered the grimness in his voice when he had told me how hopeless his life in Thailand would be without a year of American education. Knowing what he was like, I could easily imagine him taking the other boy's place—the other boy who *was* a good student—in order to get to this country and improve his life.

But how had he gotten the other boy out of the way? Was Bia worse than merely a liar and a manipulator? Could he possibly have . . . I pushed the thought away.

And what was I going to do about it? Should I tell people what I suspected so that they could investigate it? Exposing Bia! That would really be a mess. It would probably result in his being sent back to Thailand in disgrace, with no hopes left.

I remembered the glimpse of his vulnerability he had allowed me to see today and slowly shook my head. I couldn't expose him now. Whatever he had done to get here, I wasn't ready to ruin his chances for a better life.

But the only alternative was just to stand by and watch him get away with it. That would mean becoming a part of his operation myself. I was sure I'd have to help him with his homework; he'd probably want me to cheat for him. Conspiring against the school and against Mom wasn't so bad. But I'd also, indirectly, be conspiring against the innocent boy in Thailand—if he was still alive. I wasn't sure I could do that either.

And there was nobody I could turn to for help. As soon as I told one other person, Bia would be in trouble. The only person I could talk to about it was Bia himself, if I dared to confront him. But if I did, he would just deny everything. And it would make me into an enemy in his eyes.

But why should I care? Why should I worry about ruining his chances? He hadn't been concerned about the other boy's chances. Again, I wondered exactly what Bia had done to him.

And then, out of nowhere, I remembered something Dominic had said: in Thailand, people made bargains with spirits. They would ask a spirit to do them a favor and promise to give the spirit something precious in return. We had a spirit house now. Maybe I could ask the spirit, who lived in the spirit house, to help me with this dilemma.

I sighed and clucked my teeth. I was really losing it now, imagining a spirit out there. The situation was making me completely irrational. I walked up the front steps and unlocked the door.

When I saw that the mail had been picked up off the floor and neatly stacked on the hallway table I supposed that Bia might have come home already. But there was no answer when I knocked on his door, and no one inside the room when I checked. No one else was home either—Dominic must have come back after school, picked up the mail, and then gone out again.

I wandered into my room and threw myself down on the bed, wondering morosely what Bia and Gloria were doing.

My whole life was falling apart. Bia and my other friends had all turned against me. Even my hair and complexion were a mess. Nothing was going right anymore. And just a few days ago I had been fine! How had this happened? Why had everything changed?

I thought back. It all seemed to have started on Friday evening. That's when Bia got the phone call from Thailand, and then told me I was boring, and started avoiding me. That's when Gloria called to tell me Mark was with Lynette. That's when Dominic finished the spirit house.

I sat up. I was being crazy again. It *had* to be coincidence.

But it all fit together so neatly. I went over the events again, and the pattern held: everything had started to deteriorate as soon as Dominic had presented Bia with the spirit house.

What if I just imagined for a minute that spirits did exist—and that Dominic's little building had drawn a spirit from Thailand. A spirit who, for some unknown reason, was doing things to mess up my life. But a spirit who could also be bargained with, and bribed, to do good things for me.

I didn't believe in it, but what could I lose by testing it out?

I slowly got up from the bed and walked to the bathroom window. I stared out at the little brown building in the backyard, squatting on its pole like some ornate, sinister bird house—a house for carnivorous birds, raptors and scavengers, hawks and vultures, eaters of entrails. I didn't like the spirit house; I didn't want to get near it. But I felt powerfully compelled to do something. And I had to hurry. Whatever I was going to do, I wanted to be finished before Bia came home.

8

I already knew what I could give the spirit. What I didn't know was what to ask her to give me.

I was upset; I wanted to act quickly. The whole idea was crazy, I didn't really believe in it, nothing would come of it, so why not just do it on impulse? But another part of me was aware that if I rushed into this spirit business without thinking, I might make everything a lot worse.

But how could I make it worse? Why was I afraid? What was stopping me from just going down there and asking the spirit to make Bia my friend again? And to make it that he wasn't a criminal. And that he hadn't done anything bad to the real Thamrongsak. And that . . .

But could the spirit, if she existed at all, do all those things at once? What if some of them were mutually exclusive? And then I knew what was making me hesitate. It was all the stories in which people were granted wishes, and how those who wished rashly, or selfishly, or for too much, always brought on disaster.

So what could I ask for that would be effective, but also safe? What did the good people in the stories do? On the surface, it seemed that the people who benefited from wishes were those who asked for something simple and unpretentious, or something that would help another person. So all I had to do was frame my request in a way that was kindly and generous to others, and then I'd be okay too, right?

Wrong. Very quickly I remembered, with an unpleasant pang, that it *wasn't* only the nasty and grasping people who suffered as the result of a wish. Good people did too. In *Beauty and the Beast,* the selfish sisters asked their father for jewels and fancy clothes, but it was Beauty's simple request for a rose that caused all the trouble. She got through it in the end, but not Cordelia in Shakespeare's play, who was just as simple and honest with *her* father, King Lear, and they both suffered miserably because of that. Most horrible of all was *The Monkey's Paw.* The old man was a sweet and decent guy, and his innocent wish was granted—with unthinkably grisly and tragic results.

I tried not to dwell on *The Monkey's Paw.* But I couldn't help wondering if this spirit worked in the same manner: she gave you exactly what you asked for, but in an unexpectedly horrible way.

I was letting my emotions take over again. I tried to assure myself that this spirit was different, she had specific rules—you bargained with her, you paid her for your wish. And if you paid her *first,* wouldn't that protect you from any gruesome surprises? I hoped so.

But how could I be sure?

All I knew was that if there really were anything to this, it was a lot scarier than I had realized at first. Maybe I shouldn't ask for anything at all. If I did, I would have to be extremely careful, and consider all the options and ramifications. Well-meant wishes, like Dom's experiments, could backfire as easily as selfish ones.

Half an hour later I slipped out the back door, feeling self-conscious even though I knew nobody was there to see me. I approached the spirit house, my hands clenched at my sides, making an effort to maintain a steady pace. It was a beautiful day, the sun warm on my face, the yard green and bright and comfortingly familiar. I could see how small the spirit house was under the endless sky, I knew it was just a crude box hammered together by my little brother.

And I was trembling. In my mind, the shadow of the spirit house engulfed the yard, the street; its dark influence stretched all the way across the ocean from Asia.

I imagined the creature waiting inside, her head lolling upon its pulpy bed of intestines, her vacant eyes watching me approach. I paused. It was necessary to remind myself of how Bia had stolen the real Thamrongsak's rightful opportunity—and had also taken advantage of me. I plodded forward again. I stopped a foot in front of the spirit house; I pressed my palms together and deeply lowered my head.

I had thought very carefully about what to ask. I had practiced the wording. And I had not forgotten to be respectful—I had learned from Bia the Asian way of extreme politeness and deference to those of superior status. But I still made several false starts, my thoughts stumbling. Finally it dawned on me to imagine I was talking to someone who didn't speak much English—like

Bia—and that helped me to keep it slow and precise. It was important to be very clear, to make sure the spirit understood who I was, and that she did not confuse me with anyone else.

I offer you most respectful greetings, honorable one, and sincerest wishes that you are comfortable in this house my brother Dominic made for you. My name is Julie Kamen, and I beg your kind permission to hear my small request. For your consideration, I offer you something very precious to me, more precious than anything else I have to give. I offer it to you now, in hopes of earning your trust, and so that you will know how seriously I honor my part of the bargain.

What I ask you is to please let my brother Dominic learn the truth about Bia, the young man from Thailand who is staying with us, and the truth about a young man named Thamrongsak Tan-ngarmtrong. I ask that no harm come to Dominic as a result of this request or this knowledge. I ask you to ignore this request, rather than to let any harm come to Dominic.

Please understand, the precious thing I am giving you once belonged to someone else, but it was freely given to me, and it is rightfully mine. Parting with it is a great sacrifice for me. And now I freely give it to you, for considering my request. I offer you my deepest gratitude for listening to me. Thank you.

The hard part wasn't removing the chain from my neck—the loose clasp fell open at a touch. And although giving it away, now that I was really doing it, was painful enough to bring tears to my eyes, it was something I could do unflinchingly, because it made a kind of sense, and I knew that my intentions were good.

The hardest part was willing my hand to move past

the miniature porch and actually reach inside the dark open doorway of the spirit house.

I heard laughter and splashing from the neighbors' pool, the inane happy bleating of a radio, the sounds of twentieth-century America on a balmy summer day. And I stood there, my hand just outside the spirit house doorway, shivering. It was like trying to stick my hand into an open fire, or a churning garbage disposal. Did that mean I really believed there was something powerful inside, something with the head of a woman and intestines dripping from her neck? And if I *did* believe in her, then what was I getting myself into?

But I had already promised. It was too late to back out now. I squeezed my eyes shut, groaned, and thrust my hand into the darkness inside the spirit house. I dropped the chain and pendant Bia had given me, whipped my hand back, and turned and hurried across the yard.

9

"I got trampled in football," Dominic said as we were finishing the dishes that night. "The teachers treat me like an idiot. And all the girls are taller than me now, and they wear *tons* of makeup and act like they're years older. The computer room is the only good thing about junior high." He sighed and thrust in the dishwasher rack with a jarring clatter of glassware.

"Do you have to make so much noise?" I snapped, still tense. "Anyway, you'll get used to junior high," I told him, vigorously scrubbing the last pot.

"And the kids *did* think I was crazy when I told them about the spirit house. Even Harold said—"

"Dominic, you *didn't!*" I stopped suddenly, aware of the shrillness of my voice. Why shouldn't he talk about the spirit house with his own friends? "I mean, I don't want the kids to think you're weird. And right now isn't the time to, you know, tempt fate. I don't want . . . anything to happen to you."

"Huh?" He looked at me, wide-eyed. "Tempt fate?

What do you mean, you don't want anything to happen to me?"

I turned away to rinse the pot, accused by his innocent and earnest expression. How would he feel if he knew what I had asked the spirit, that I had involved him in it? Guilt gnawed at me. I pushed it away, telling myself I was overreacting. "Oh, I don't know, Dom. I guess I just didn't have a very good day myself."

"Yeah? Something about Bia, right? I wondered why he was looking at you in that funny way all during supper."

I almost dropped the pot. Bia had been watching me? I hadn't noticed, since I had been doing my best not to look at him. But maybe he had seen how nervous I was. Maybe he was suspicious. He *could* have seen me standing by the spirit house this afternoon; he and Dominic were both home, up in Dominic's room, when I had come inside.

"How did he *really* do at school, anyway?" Dominic asked me. "Couldn't tell anything from what he said."

I tried to control my voice. "The kids liked him," I said, thinking of the afternoon he had spent with Gloria. I had refused to ask him about it, carefully avoiding him. "And you'll do fine too, Dom," I added. "As long as you don't turn people off by talking about . . . about weird things."

"Yeah, well, the computer room *is* pretty cool. And as soon as I get access to the mainframe I might be able to have some fun. It shouldn't be too hard to get through. And you know what? The junior high and the high school both have the same mainframe, I'm pretty sure of it."

"Really? You mean you could get access to high school files—classified data?"

"Uh-huh." He nodded proudly. "I really think I could do it."

"That's . . . interesting." How could Bia take advantage of that—and of Dominic? The possibilities were endless, for someone unscrupulous like Bia.

But at least Dominic's practicality was beginning to nudge me into a more levelheaded state of mind. Suddenly I felt a little embarrassed at the stupidity of what I had done this afternoon. How could I worry that leaving Bia's pendant inside the spirit house would put me or Dominic in danger? The real danger to Dominic was that Bia might get him in trouble, by using Dominic's computer knowledge to fix his transcript here. "Hey, Dom."

"Yeah?" he said, wiping off the counter.

"You better not say anything about—"

Bia appeared in the kitchen doorway.

I shut my mouth and squatted down to put the pot into the cupboard.

"What, Julie?" Dominic said.

"Nothing. Forget it." I had been about to warn Dominic not to tell Bia about the computer connection to the high school. I hoped I would have another chance—it was just the kind of thing Dominic liked to brag about, and Bia was always encouraging him to talk about computers.

"Hey, Bia, you'll never guess what I found out today," Dominic said. "The computers at my school are—"

"Dominic!"

They both turned and looked at me, surprised by my tone of voice.

I tried to laugh, cursing myself for not warning Dominic earlier. "I bet Bia's dying for a cigarette, Dom," I said lightly. "You can talk later. Come on, Bia." I hurried out of the kitchen before Dominic could say anything else, and Bia came with me.

Why wasn't he avoiding me, as he had done all weekend? What if he had seen me by the spirit house, and asked me about it? At least I wouldn't have to be confronted with the spirit house and Bia together, now that he had developed the habit of smoking on the front porch.

But Bia walked past me at the front door. "Hey," I said. "Aren't you . . ."

"Something wrong, Julie?"

I swallowed. "No. Nothing." I didn't want him to think I had any reason to avoid the backyard. I walked with him through the house, out the sliding doors at the back and down the steps into the night, my skin prickling, urging myself to *stop* being foolish, once and for all.

What was there to be afraid of? I didn't seriously believe in the spirit. And even if she did exist—unlikely as that was—I had wished safely. My request wasn't selfish; it was possible that it could be granted without any benefit to me at all. But unselfishness wasn't the only reason I had asked her to let Dominic be the one to learn the truth about Bia. I had done that because I knew Dominic would deal with it better than I could. I didn't want the knowledge in my hands alone. I had already lied to Mom and Dad to keep them from learning about Bia's room in Bangkok. If I knew more, I might also conceal it—either out of concern for Bia or because he might manipulate me again.

But Dominic was too young, and too bluntly honest, to play games with truth. Once he learned the truth, whatever it was, his only concern would be to do the fair and decent thing. And I didn't *think* I was using Dominic or putting him in danger. I had specified that no harm should come to him.

Still, I would have preferred to be on the front porch. Especially when I realized, as I walked with Bia across the lawn, what I had left out of the wish: I had forgotten to ask the spirit that no harm should come to me.

"You angry at me, Julie?" Bia said.

But *he* was the one who had been avoiding *me* all weekend! "What makes you think I'm angry?" I asked him, trying to sound casual.

"You don't wear Buddha pendant I give you."

That's why he had been staring at me during supper. A shiver worked its way from my stomach up along my spine. "I . . . I just took it off."

"Put where? In bag? In pocket?"

It was all I could do not to turn and look directly at the spirit house. And because I was scared, Bia's cross-examination made me angry. "What difference does it make where I put it? It's mine. You gave it to me. I can do anything I want with it."

"Only want you to understand, Julie," he said, his serious voice coming out of the darkness, the burning end of the cigarette closing in on his fingertips, the only part of him I could see. "Very holy thing. Must be careful. Good luck if wear. But if put in low place, then not good for you, Julie. Better if you wear. You understand?" He flicked away the cigarette, a bright streak arching toward the spirit house, without turning his face from me.

Was he really worried I would bring bad luck on myself by not treating the pendant carefully enough? Or was it simply that his feelings were hurt because I had taken off this very special gift from him? "I would never be careless with it, believe me. It's very special to me."

"Then where you put?" His face flickered in the flame of his gold lighter, though his eyes remained shadowed. "In bag? In pocket? Or some other place?" He turned, drawing deeply on his new cigarette, and gazed directly at the spirit house for a long moment. He looked slowly back at me. "Where, Julie?"

I couldn't answer, panicking. He watched me. Leaves rustled, a many-voiced whisper that swelled and gradually subsided.

"What you ask spirit for, Julie?" he said, moving suddenly toward me. He squeezed his right hand around my arm. I jerked away from him, my heart racing. He tightened his hold. His grip was very strong.

He *must* have seen me standing by the spirit house. And now that the pendant was missing, it was only natural that he'd suspect what I had done. "What you ask spirit for?" he repeated, his voice tense but strangely hushed.

How could I have forgotten to ask the spirit to protect me? "Let go of me!" I struggled to pull my arm away. "You're hurting me!"

"You not tell me?" He squeezed harder.

"Not telling you *what?*" My voice cracked; in another second I'd be crying.

"*Mai pen rai!*" he said, the foreign words quick and biting. He flung my arm away so suddenly that I staggered backward and almost fell. "*Mai pen rai.* Do not care *what* you do!" He spoke with contempt, breathing hard. "You hear me, Julie? You not my friend. You my enemy. You hear?"

"W-What?" I said, rubbing my arm, my throat tightening. It was so unlike Bia to speak in this direct, harsh way that his words had a kind of nightmarish unreality.

"Listen. I am not care about you." He looked directly at the spirit house, raising his voice. "Am not care about you, Julie Kamen. Care about Gloria, care about Lynette, care about other girl. But not you. You are liar."

"Liar? *You're* calling *me* a liar?" I was so angry that I didn't care how loud my voice was. "*You're* the one who lies to everybody. You don't think I noticed that? You don't think I know what you—" I gulped the words back. Furious as I was, I was also too afraid of him now to let him know what I suspected. I started to turn away.

"Julie."

The way he said it made me look back. He was facing the light from the deck now, I could see the fragile line of his mouth, the same lost, vulnerable expression I had noticed at school this morning. But he said nothing more.

"You're *crazy!*" I blurted out. But now there was an edge of guilt to my anger. Whatever his motivation for giving me the pendant, it had been a very great sacrifice for him. And I had discarded his gift—in an effort to trap him.

But maybe it hadn't really been mine to give, and the spirit knew that. Then it wouldn't matter if I took it away from her. If I gave it to Bia, then I could stop worrying about what I had wished. Suddenly I wanted no part of any bargain with the spirit.

I hurried to the spirit house. "Here, Bia. Take it. It

really belongs to you." I thrust my hand inside the dark little doorway, groping for the pendant.

The spirit house was empty.

10

The hairs on the back of my neck lifted. But I did not remove my hand from the spirit house. My fingers raked across the bare boards. "It's not here!" I peered frantically through the doorway. Inside there was no glint of chain or pendant, only darkness.

"You give. Spirit take," Bia's quiet voice came from behind me. "Too late change."

"No! It's not *possible!*" I dropped to my knees, pawing at the grass underneath the spirit house. The pendant wasn't there. "*You* took it out!" I accused him.

"Don't be stupid. If I take, I not say anything."

That made sense. If he had taken it he would have kept quiet about the pendant, instead of calling attention to it. And when could he have taken it? I had been pretty distracted, but it seemed to me that he had been up in Dominic's room from the time I had put it in the spirit house until Mom called them to supper. I jumped to my feet. "I don't want to talk about it, think about it anymore, ever!"

He shrugged, tall and elegant, and glanced at the spirit

house. "Just remember—I not your friend now, Julie."

I turned and ran; I reached the deck just as Dominic was stepping out through the glass doors. "Telephone, Julie," he said, and then stopped, staring at me. "What's the matter?"

"Nothing."

"Dominic!" Bia called from the yard. "What you want to tell me before?"

"Oh, that's right." Dominic stepped to the edge of the deck. "Guess what I found out today? About the computers at my school, and at the high—"

"Dom, wait, don't!"

But it was too late. "Computer?" Bia was saying, walking toward him across the lawn. "Computer at your school and high school? What about computer?"

"Oh, Dominic," I groaned. He didn't even hear me. He was already hurrying to tell Bia his discovery.

But I was more worried about the pendant than the computers now. I trudged inside, wondering if I was going crazy. Had I only *imagined* putting the pendant inside the spirit house? But that wasn't possible—I knew I had done it. Maybe one of the neighbor kids had stolen it. That had to be it. Or else a bird or squirrel had taken it. They liked bright shiny things, didn't they? "It was a bird," I whispered, trying to convince myself.

Because if it wasn't a bird, or a neighbor kid—then the spirit was real. I was trapped in a bargain with her.

And on top of everything else, Bia was my enemy. He had told me in so many words. And what would he do—implacable and hostile now—if he ever found out what I suspected about him? I looked behind me before I picked up the phone.

"Julie? It's . . . me," Mark said, uncharacteristically hesitant. "I just wanted to say, could we . . . go somewhere and talk?"

"Talk?" I said stupidly.

"Yes. I . . . well, I made a mistake. I was hoping you'd let me explain."

"Explain? Why don't you explain to Lynette?" I asked him, ready to slam down the receiver.

"Please, Julie. I'm sorry. If only you'd give me a chance. I'd really like things to be—"

"What's the matter? Did Lynette stand you up or something?"

"No, she didn't. I just . . . came to my senses, I guess. I don't know what was the matter with me. I don't blame you for being mad. I deserve it. It's just that I'd really like to see you."

"Wait a minute. Let me get this straight. You're not interested in Lynette anymore? You want to go out with me now?"

"Yes. Can I please see you tonight?"

It was a little hard to believe this was actually happening; it wasn't like Mark to be so *inhumanly* humble and apologetic. Why his sudden change in attitude toward me?

But I might as well see where this was leading. Maybe my life wasn't falling apart after all. Maybe I had a chance of being popular again.

I wasn't going to make it *too* easy for him, though, after the way he had treated me today. "I'm kind of busy right now," I said slowly. "But *maybe* I could think about meeting you."

"Just for a few minutes, Julie. Please?"

I held the receiver away and stared at it quizzically.

This was Mark? I was very curious now. "Well, I guess I could find the time," I said, trying to sound offhand. "You might as well pick me up now."

"*Thank* you, Julie." His voice was flooded with relief. "I'll be there in fifteen minutes."

I brushed my teeth and fixed my hair and makeup. The pimples seemed to have been a false alarm; they had shrunk down to almost nothing, hardly visible anymore. My hair looked better than it had all day.

Another surprise—Mom made no objections about it being a school night when I told her I was going out with Mark. "Have a good time," she said, smiling at me. "You look nice, Julie."

I walked slowly down the stairs. Mom *never* told me I looked nice. What was the matter with everybody tonight?

Last year I would have run outside when Mark's red Thunderbird pulled up. Tonight I was thinking about things. I waited for him to park and walk to the house and ring the bell. "You look great, Julie," he said, smiling bashfully when I opened the door. "This is really nice of you."

In the car, he said he just wanted to drive around and talk, and I shrugged, as though it didn't matter to me. I hoped Mom and Dad didn't notice the squeal of his tires as he shot down the street.

"I'm sorry I didn't call you sooner," he began. "But Lynette was at the airport to meet me, and you weren't, and she said you—"

"You didn't call Lynette?"

He looked puzzled. "No. Lynette met me at the airport."

It hurt me to think of Lynette deliberately trying to take him away from me, and Gloria being so eager to tell me he was with Lynette. These were my best friends? "Go on," I said.

"Then, tonight, Lynette was getting on my nerves. And I just kept thinking about you. It was a dumb mistake, going out with her. It won't happen again, Julie. Now I really know how much I want to be with you."

I smiled at him, beginning to feel elated. Mark was ordinary—but he was also open and honest. Everyone liked him. And now not only did he want to go out with me again; he was telling me he liked me better than ever. After the bleakness of the last few days, life was starting to look pretty good.

And when I got home that night, Lynette phoned to apologize.

The next night after supper there was a light knock on the door of my room. "Come in," I said.

Bia pushed open the door. "Can explain English essay for me, please? Take only minute." He spoke in a monotone, his manner dignified and reserved.

My first impulse was to tell him to go ask Lynette to help him—he had spent the afternoon with her. But as I was about to speak I noticed again that shadow of vulnerability in the set of his mouth. I couldn't say no. "Sure. Bring it here."

It didn't take a minute, it took hours. I practically had to write his essay for him. And after that, there were other subjects. Bia understood almost nothing of what the teachers had said in class. It began to dawn on me, with a trapped, hopeless feeling, that his survival at school depended on me spending every spare minute helping him.

We worked grimly until ten o'clock, when Bia said, "Take break. Call Lynette, before too late. Back in five minute."

I felt an angry tightening in my stomach. "Sure," I said, keeping my voice under control. As soon as he was out of the room I furiously snapped a pencil in half and hurled it to the floor.

Mark drove me to school the next day. Several times he told me how nice I looked. He carried my books when we walked into the building together in front of the other kids. It was a very different entrance from yesterday.

Gloria and Lynette were both desperate to talk to me. I was polite and distant to them at first. But they were both so earnestly apologetic, and so anxious to be forgiven, that I couldn't go on holding a grudge against them. Several senior boys who had never noticed me before made a point of coming over and talking with me. Gloria and Lynette were very impressed.

I felt so exhilarated by how well everything went for me at school that I didn't even mind helping Bia with his homework that night. I was also aware that the better he did in school, the less likely he would be to try to use Dominic's computer knowledge to fix his grades— helping him was a way of protecting Dominic. I spent one or two hours working with him the next night, and the next, and it soon became a pattern. He never forgot to thank me, but he was more remote and formal with me than ever.

And when we weren't studying, Bia spent time with

Gloria, and Lynette, and then Gloria, and then Lynette, and sometimes Lynda or Gayle, and then Gloria again, and then again Lynette.

Yet he didn't seem at all self-satisfied by his conquests. He betrayed no emotions to me, but I sensed that he was unhappy. He wasn't eating much. After a week or so, I began to notice stains on the knees of his pants. He seemed tired all the time, slumping. There were dark circles under his eyes. Despite my help, he wasn't doing well in school.

At night, I could hear him coughing in his room; he was smoking more than ever. And I saw that he was lighting his cigarettes with ordinary matches now. What had happened to the gold lighter he had been so proud of? I was curious, but I didn't dare ask him. Partly it was because he was so chilly and unapproachable. But I was also afraid that if I mentioned the lighter, it might bring up the subject of the other valuable possession he no longer had. I didn't want him to ask me again what I had done with the pendant, or what I had asked the spirit. I was afraid of what he might do if he thought I had any suspicions about him.

And late one night I noticed, from the upstairs bathroom window, that the pinpoint of light in the backyard was not a cigarette, but something burning on the spirit house porch. I quietly pushed up the screen and leaned out. The trees shivered; leaves drifted down. Bia was kneeling in front of the spirit house, his head bent almost to the ground. I felt a chill, understanding the stains on his pants. Was he trying to get help from the spirit by praying to her, by burning incense? Had he given her his lighter?

When I got into bed at night, in the short time before I would fall into deep, restful sleep, I thought about the missing pendant. What had happened to it? Someone *must* have taken it out of the spirit house—that was the only rational explanation. I didn't think it was Bia; if he had taken it he certainly wouldn't have asked me about it, drawing suspicion onto himself. It had to have been one of the neighbor children, or a bird or an animal.

I also wondered when, if ever, we were going to learn the truth about Bia. Was the wish still in effect? Or had my bargain with the spirit been nullified because the pendant had been taken away from her? I *had* given the pendant to the spirit, purposely, and had not taken it back myself. By any logic that made sense, my bargain with her still held.

How long was it going to take for the wish to work? I was very impatient to find out all about Bia. Yet at the same time, in the back of my mind, I was also apprehensive about what he would do if I ever *did* learn the truth about him.

Aside from that worry, my life was close to perfect. Mark drove me to school every day and phoned me every evening. He carried my books between classes. And he did not go out with any other girls. He was more devoted to me than he had ever been last year. I didn't understand it—but I loved it!

"You're so lucky about Mark," Lynette said wanly on the soccer field one wet day. "He never even *looks* at any other girls."

"I know," I said smugly.

She turned away from me and coughed, her hand over her mouth. "*Bia* still goes out with Gloria. God, I hate her!" She could talk freely, since Gloria was sick at home today—the two of them were bitter enemies now. Lynette pushed a greasy tangle of hair out of her eyes. "*You* know Bia, Julie. What can I do to make him—"

"Quick, here it comes!" I interrupted her.

Lynette lurched toward the ball and tripped and fell in the mud. I trampled on her hair, reached the ball, and kicked it with a resounding smack. It sailed across the goal line. Everybody cheered me—including Lynette.

The next day Lynette was home sick. "God, my hair looks like seaweed!" Gloria groaned, staring into the school bathroom mirror. She blew her nose juicily on a piece of toilet paper. "And these pimples! I've never had them so bad. Your skin looks great, Julie," she said wistfully. "What's the secret?"

"There's no secret. I'm not doing anything different." It was the truth. "It just looks like this."

The bell rang. Out in the hallway Gloria sighed. "Did Bia call Lynette last night?" she asked me fervently, in her wispy little voice. "Come on Julie, you can tell me. Does he talk about her a lot?"

"No, he doesn't talk about her a lot. He doesn't talk about *you* much, either," I added.

"Gloria." Miss Becker stopped her in the hallway. "Why weren't you in class today?"

"I'm sorry. I was late—I couldn't sleep last night."

Becker shook her head. "Not acceptable," she said. "Your performance in general this year has been atrocious. I'm going to have to send a note to your mother."

"No, *please* don't!" Gloria begged her. "She's already crabbing at me all the time. If you—"

Becker didn't want to hear it. She turned to me,

beaming. "Your last paper was *excellent,* Julie. Be prepared for me to read it to the class today."

When I got home from school that day, no one else was there. But, as always, the mail was neatly stacked on the hall table. I wondered about it. But I never could remember to ask Mom or Dad or Dominic which one of them was doing it.

The following Saturday night Mark took me out for an expensive dinner. "That guy Bia," he said, as he paid the bill with the credit card his parents had given him. "He'd better watch it."

"What do you mean?"

"Everybody's getting a little tired of the way he's so stuck-up and superior."

"Gloria and Lynette don't seem to be turned off," I pointed out.

Mark shrugged. "Those dogs? I wasn't talking about them. It's the cool kids who are sick of his attitude. And the teachers aren't too thrilled with him either. I overheard Kimball telling him he wasn't going to pass math."

I wasn't helping Bia with math. But I knew he wasn't doing well in English.

"But why am I talking about him?" Mark cleared his throat. "There's something I want to give you," he said shyly. He took a small velvet box out of his jacket pocket and pushed it toward me across the table. "Here. Open it."

It was a gold bracelet with our initials engraved on it. Mark fastened it awkwardly around my wrist, blushing a little. "Thanks, Mark," I said. "It's beautiful."

But I was thinking about Bia giving me the pendant, the jade Buddha pendant that had disappeared inside the spirit house. Was that why things were going so well for me now—the spirit was rewarding me for giving it to her?

And was the spirit also the reason things were going so badly for Bia?

11

Bia *had* been uncomfortable talking about spirits from the beginning. He had been extremely upset when Dominic had given him the spirit house.

I was still thinking about it when I got home that night. Had Bia offended the spirit? Was it something he might have done in Thailand—something relating to the real Thamrongsak? Maybe the spirit he had offended in Thailand had somehow been drawn here by the spirit house. He did seem to be trying to placate the spirit now—without apparent results.

And I remembered what Dominic had said about how you could get in trouble if you made a bargain with the spirit and then didn't keep your part of it. I seemed to recall Dominic asking Bia about that. But I couldn't remember what, if anything, Bia had answered.

I wandered into the family room, too preoccupied to think of hiding Mark's bracelet from Mom.

Mom was reading and Dad was watching television. Mom smiled at me. "You look lovely, Julie," she said. "Your hair, that dress—everything."

"Thanks," I said. I sank listlessly into a chair and stretched my feet out in front of me, which always used to irritate Mom. "Is Bia home?"

"Who knows?" Mom said, with a disdainful shrug. Then she closed her book and stared at my wrist. "Julie! That bracelet! Did Mark give it to you?"

I groaned inwardly. Mom thought it was cheap and demeaning for women to accept expensive presents from men. She also didn't believe in people my age getting too serious. Now she'd start lecturing me.

"Well," I said. "He . . . It's nothing. No big deal."

"What do you mean, nothing? It's *beautiful,*" Mom said. "Let me see."

I limply held out my arm. Mom studied the bracelet closely. "It's really good-looking, Julie. And obviously expensive. Mark must think a lot of you."

Dad smiled fondly. "Shows he has good judgment."

"And you're showing good judgment too, Julie," Mom said. "I don't just mean about Mark. I'm proud of the way you're handling things in general. You're bringing home good grades, even though you're spending all that study time helping Bia. You've become so well-organized."

"I'm not sure I like the way he's letting you help him so much, though," Dad said.

Mom sighed. "Yes. It seems to me Bia's taking advantage of you, Julie. I was expecting more of him. I'm afraid he's turning out to be a disappointment."

Should I tell them now that I was pretty sure he wasn't the real Thamrongsak? That he had done something unscrupulous to get to this country? They'd probably believe me. I couldn't seem to do anything wrong these days. And Bia couldn't do anything right.

But I didn't mention it. In spite of everything he had done, I just couldn't bring myself to destroy Bia's chance for a better future. If I did expose him, he would have to leave, and I wasn't ready for that yet. I wanted to find out the truth first. I needed solid evidence for my suspicions. Then I'd decide what to do.

I was also a little afraid to mention what I suspected about him. What if Bia overheard me? I didn't want him to get the idea I knew something that could upset his future. If he did, he'd try to stop me—maybe in the same way he'd stopped Thamrongsak. I needed to know what had happened to Thamrongsak before I said anything.

I was still thinking about the spirit as I drifted off to sleep that night.

I had asked the spirit to let Dominic discover the truth about Bia—assuming I would then learn it from him. But I didn't see much of Dominic these days. I was busy, and so was Dom. He and Bia still spent some time at his computer. But now Dominic often stayed late after school, apparently working at the computer room there, leaving his computer at home free for Bia's use. About the only time I saw Dominic was at meals, when only public things could be discussed. We were never alone together. I began to wonder if that in itself might be odd. Was Dominic avoiding me? And what was he doing at the school computers?

The first Saturday in October, Bia, with Dominic's help, cooked a Thai meal, and Mark came over for dinner. I was amazed at how deftly Bia had put together five different dishes in just a couple of hours, after he had rushed back from the store with an armload of weird packages. He made Thai fried chicken, curried pork, shrimp with vegetables and cashew nuts, cold beef salad, another salad of mostly unrecognizable vegetables, and rice to go with everything. The salads especially were works of art, the vegetables cut into flower shapes, scallions curled like chrysanthemums, everything beautifully arranged on the serving plates.

"Hope you like," Bia said politely as he sat down. He looked gaunt in his oversize red and black shirt. "Try not make too *pet* for American taste."

"Pet?" Mark asked him.

"It means spicy-hot," Dominic said. "That's why there's *two* pitchers of ice water."

Dad choked and gulped down water after his first tentative bite. "You're trying to tell me this isn't *hot?*" he gasped, dabbing sweat from his brow with a paper napkin.

"In Thailand, three times more hot," Bia explained. "This very, very mild."

Soon, rivulets were meandering down Dad's bald head, soaking his collar. Bia was the only one who didn't sweat through piles of paper napkins and didn't need many glasses of water. But hot as the food was, it was also extremely delicious. Then I noticed that Dominic and I were the only ones gobbling it down; no one else seemed to like it. Were their negative feelings about Bia affecting their taste buds too?

Dominic kept telling Bia how good the food was, since nobody else was complimenting him about it. I liked the food, but I didn't say anything. I was thinking, wondering why Dominic was so concerned with Bia's feelings. Was it possible that Dominic *was* learning about Bia, and not telling me? And how could I find out without making Bia suspicious?

I studied Dominic. Like me, Dom had always allowed his emotions to show; he had never been a liar. But now I remembered how well he kept the secret of the spirit house while he was building it. That was unusual for him. Had he changed somehow? Had he suddenly developed the ability to hide his feelings? Had he become more like Bia—cool, polite, nonconfrontational, keeping his real emotions to himself?

Then I remembered another odd thing that had been happening that I had not asked anyone about. And now I was too curious to be careful; I just blurted it out. "Every day when I come home, even though nobody else is here, somebody's already gone through the mail. It's not on the floor, it's piled on the table. It must be you, Dom. What are you looking for?"

"Excuse, please." Bia got up from the table and left the room.

"The mail?" Dominic said, sounding honestly baffled. "Why would I do that? I haven't ordered any equipment."

"Then who's doing it?" I demanded, looking around the table.

Dad shook his head, blinking sweat out of his eyes. "I'm sure there's some simple explanation," Mom said. "They've probably changed the delivery schedule. Maybe it's coming early now, before Dad or I go to work, and one of us has been going through it."

Bia returned and handed Dad a bath towel. Dad barely looked at him. "Thanks. This is just what I need—eating this stuff," Dad said.

"But if one of you was going through the mail, wouldn't you *know* you were doing it?"

"Not necessarily." Dad wiped his head with the towel.

"I'm always preoccupied in the morning, thinking about work. Sorting the mail is one of those things I do automatically."

"More to eat?" Bia offered. "Plenty for everybody."

He had hardly touched the small amount of food he had served himself.

Mark smiled at me. "Can I serve you something?" he asked.

"No thanks," I said absentmindedly. One of them had to be lying about the mail.

Usually Mark and I drove around for a while after school before he took me home. But on the following Monday I wanted to be the first one in the house, to check on the mail. I told Mark I didn't feel good and asked him to take me straight home. He didn't question it, though I had never looked, or felt, healthier. He obeyed immediately, full of concern, hoping I wasn't getting sick.

Lynette was sitting in her car in front of our house, the motor turned off. I looked in through the driver's seat window. Her face was an ugly pink from the sunlamp she'd been using to try to get rid of her pimples. "Hi. What's happening?" I said.

"Same as usual." She paused to blow her nose. "Bia always drops off his books and changes clothes right after school." She sneezed, grabbing for another tissue. "Oh, this *cold!*" she moaned. "Don't get too close, Julie. I'd feel *terrible* if I gave it to you." I hurried inside.

And found Bia in the front hallway, going through the mail.

12

I moved toward him, really angry now. "What are you looking for in the mail, Bia? What are you afraid is coming? What don't you want anybody else to see?"

"Not making sense, Julie," he said, calmly putting down the envelopes and moving past me toward the door.

His casual dismissal of me was infuriating. "You're lying!" I shouted at his back. I had caught him in the act, and he still refused to admit it. His lying to me now was an insult. Did he think I was a complete idiot? The words spilled out, beyond my control. "You're lying, and you're *not* going to get away with it! You're looking for a letter from the *real* Thamrongsak, aren't you!"

His head jerked back around as though he had been slapped. He stared at me, his chin lifted, his lips pressed tightly together. I could see the veins on his neck. "Be careful, Julie," he said slowly. "Do not want anything happen to you. Be very careful." He held my eyes for a long moment. Then he stepped outside and pulled the door shut behind him with a gentle click.

I stood without moving, the silence of the house swelling around me. I had just told Bia what I suspected about him. And nobody else was home. What if Bia didn't drive away with Lynette? I couldn't lock him out; he had his own key.

I dropped my books and looked quickly through the envelopes, just in case he *did* come right back in. There was nothing unusual, of course. If there had been, Bia had already found and taken it.

My anger returned. *He's* not *going to get away with it!* I swore to myself, and rushed up the stairs to Mom's study.

I half expected the letter and the photo from Thamrongsak to be missing, but they were still where I had left them the day of Bia's arrival. I was familiar with Bia's handwriting now; I *might* be able to prove that this letter had been written by somebody else.

I studied the photo. Bia was thinner than when he'd arrived, as thin as the boy in the picture. And now that I knew him better, it was clear to me that this was not a photo of Bia. I could see that Thamrongsak's face was shorter and wider, with a different bone structure. His nose was flatter than Bia's, his chin less prominent. And Thamrongsak was squinting—the way people who need glasses squint when they don't have them.

Thamrongsak was probably too poor to afford glasses. I stared at his scrawny, homely face. And I was ashamed. *I* hadn't wanted Thamrongsak to come, out of pure selfishness, because he was funny-looking and not cool. I had been very relieved when this handsome and slippery impostor showed up—*he* wouldn't jeopardize my precious status! I was almost as bad as Bia.

But not quite. I hadn't wanted Thamrongsak to come, but I hadn't done anything to prevent it. And Bia must have. He had succeeded in taking Thamrongsak's place, and he had fooled everybody except me.

Maybe not everybody. There was also the spirit.

The spirit seemed to be working against Bia. And he was afraid of her. For weeks he'd been making a big effort to appease her. Was it possible that there was some connection between the spirit and whatever it was Bia had done to Thamrongsak?

I thought back. As soon as Dominic had presented Bia with the spirit house, the phone call from Thailand had come—and Bia's personality had changed. Suddenly he was nervous, and hostile toward me.

And the very next Monday he had started going through the mail.

The phone call *had* to have some connection with the letter he was looking for. I puzzled over it. The person on the phone had asked for Thamrongsak. But Thamrongsak's family must know he hadn't come here; they wouldn't call asking for him. So who would?

Maybe somebody who was in on the scheme, who knew Bia was pretending to be Thamrongsak. The call must have been from a cohort of Bia's. Telling him what? Telling him something that resulted in him going through the mail, looking for a letter that he didn't want us to see—probably because it would expose him. And who would want to expose Bia? Thamrongsak's family, of course. Maybe they had found out what he had done and had written to us about him. And Bia's friend knew it, and called to warn him to be on the lookout for the letter. That made sense. The more I thought about it, the more sure I was.

But what if he had already found and disposed of the incriminating letter? What if he succeeded in pacifying the spirit with gifts and prayer? It was intolerable that Bia might still get away with it. Not for one more minute would I be tricked into helping him! I couldn't wait to tell him to do his homework himself tonight. What would he do then? His charming manner wouldn't keep the teachers from flunking him. Whatever he had learned about computers wouldn't help him when I told Mom and Dad and Mrs. Keating and everybody else the truth.

What was I waiting for? It was clear to me that he was not the boy in the photo, and that his handwriting was different from Thamrongsak's. And I had more evidence now—I'd caught him going through the mail. I accused him, and he threatened me. Why shouldn't I start telling people about him right this minute? I rushed to my room and dialed Gloria's number.

She answered on the first ring. "Oh . . . hi, Julie," she whispered, so faintly I could barely hear her.

"What's the matter with your voice?"

"It's this stupid laryngitis," Gloria squeaked miserably. "It just won't go away. And I've got this facial mask on. It makes it kind of hard to move my lips. I'm *praying* it might do something about these hideous pimples. It's so *unfair*. As soon as I meet Bia, I break out worse than I ever did in my life. I feel like one big wound." She sighed, and then cackled weakly. "Well, at least *Lynette's* skin is just as bad as mine; I have that to be thankful for. Anyway, was there something you wanted to tell me?"

I didn't want to tell her now. "I have to go," I said, as another piece of the pattern fell into place. I hung up slowly.

Gloria and Lynette had suddenly developed ferocious pimples; my skin was clearer than it had ever been. Gloria and Lynette were sick a lot and not sleeping well; I was full of energy, in great shape, sleeping like a baby. Gloria and Lynette were being hassled by teachers and parents; everyone was treating *me* like Miss Perfection.

Gloria and Lynette were going out with Bia; I was his enemy.

It hit me like a punch in the stomach, and I sank down onto my bed. The logic was irrefutable. The spirit was Bia's enemy, doing whatever she could to punish him. And hurting his friends would be just one more effective way for her to get at him. It would add to Bia's troubles to see those he cared about suffering. It would also eventually drive everyone away from him, once they figured out how unhealthy it was to be his friend—and how rewarding to be his enemy.

Telling me I was boring, up in his room, wasn't enough. But three days later, he had said I was his enemy, in so many words, right outside the spirit house. And ever since I had been blessed with every imaginable gift—looks, health, grades, popularity. The pattern was so clear that it no longer seemed at all crazy to believe in the spirit; it seemed crazy not to. So wasn't it my duty to warn Gloria and Lynette to steer clear of Bia, before even worse things started happening to them?

I shook my head and groaned. They'd never believe

me. Neither would I, in their position. If I wanted to protect Gloria and Lynette, the way to do it wasn't to tell them a spirit was out to get them. If it seemed that they really were in danger, I would have to find some other way to separate them from Bia.

From out on the street, I heard the sound of Lynette's car starting up and driving away.

What was Bia feeling? Was he at all guilty? Obviously he didn't feel guilty enough to leave Gloria and Lynette alone. A decent person would have dropped them as soon as he saw how the spirit was punishing them because of him. Instead, he was just letting it happen.

But why should he worry about Gloria and Lynette if he hadn't worried about Thamrongsak? I thought of Thamrongsak's letter and felt another wave of compassion for him. I got up and looked at it again. "I work always very hard at my studies and my job after school. But many times I am crying, because still no chance for a better life, as my family are so poor. Now, because of your help, I can have hope. . . ."

The words blurred; I couldn't go on reading it. I wiped my eyes and picked up the photo. It seemed to me now that there was an expression of sad bafflement on Thamrongsak's face. What had happened to him was so unfair!

I dropped the photo on Mom's desk and went back and stretched out miserably on my bed. I couldn't help feeling partly responsible for his misfortune. I hadn't *done* anything to hurt him, but I had *hoped* something would happen to prevent him from coming—mainly because I was afraid of what people like Mark and Gloria and Lynette would think of him.

Was there any way to help him? I didn't know what

Bia had done to him. But if Thamrongsak were still alive and well, proving Bia was an impostor might give him another chance. So why hadn't I told Gloria that Bia was a fake? Partly because I had realized that the photo and letter from Thamrongsak still wouldn't be enough evidence to convince her. And what would be enough? The letter Bia was trying to snatch was what would do it—if he hadn't found it already.

But if he hadn't, he would now be even more determined to get his hands on it, after what I said to him in the hallway. Why hadn't I kept my mouth shut? I actually accused him of looking for a letter from the real Thamrongsak! He'd make sure I never found it.

And he'd try to stop me from telling anybody what I knew.

I felt my heart pounding in my neck, really scared now. I remembered the strength in Bia's hand when he grabbed me outside the spirit house, and the startling malice of what he said to me that night. I thought of the grim, steely expression on his face a few minutes ago when he warned me in his soft voice to be careful.

He was praying to the spirit often, burning incense; I was sure he had given her his lighter. If he got the spirit on his side, I'd be in a whole lot of trouble. And Bia would do whatever was necessary to keep me quiet. He didn't have much compunction. He had coolly stolen Thamrongsak's only chance. He wasn't bothered by what was happening to Gloria and Lynette—and he supposedly *liked* them. He didn't like me.

And I had just let him know how dangerous I was to him. What was to stop him from unleashing the spirit's hatefulness against me? The spirit was being good to me now. But I had made no bargain with her to protect me. When would the spirit start after me? As soon as Bia paid her enough, that's when.

Wind rattled the window. But I thought I heard another sound too. Was it a footstep, or just a normal creak? Was I really alone in the house? Maybe Bia hadn't driven away with Lynette, but just talked to her for a while and then came back inside when she left. I wanted to call out, to see if he was there, but I felt paralyzed. He was my enemy. His whole future depended on shutting me up.

Dominic. Maybe I could get him on my side, tell him what I had figured out. He might pay more attention to the evidence I had than Gloria would. Once he knew what was going on, how could he refuse to help me?

And maybe he already knew more than I realized. I had asked the spirit to let Dominic find out the truth about Bia. And now I knew how effective the spirit could be. Maybe she had arranged things so that Dominic had information I didn't. Together we might be able to put the whole story together and come up with solid, airtight proof. Once everybody else knew the truth about Bia, I'd be a lot safer.

But first I would have to find some way to get Dominic alone, where there was no chance Bia could overhear us. That wouldn't be easy. Dominic and I hardly ever saw each other anymore. Bia would be suspicious if we sneaked off alone.

But if we weren't at home, how could Bia know? I was pretty sure Dominic was at the junior high computer room right now, and it was still early. Mark would drop everything to drive me there as soon as I asked him to. And I wanted to get out of the house. I didn't like not knowing if Bia was here or not.

I quietly closed the door of my room and called Mark. "Pick me up right away. I need a ride to the junior high," I told him.

Mark laughed. "You think I'm your chauffeur? Forget it!" He hung up.

I stared at the phone. What was the matter with Mark? I hadn't done anything to make him angry at me. But there wasn't time to worry about it now. I had to get out of here and talk to Dominic. I could walk to the junior high.

The house was so dark that it seemed much later than midafternoon. A storm must be coming. Out in the dim hallway, trying to ignore the feeling of being watched, I peered cautiously through the open doorway into Bia's room. He wasn't there. I stood still, listening. There were no footsteps upstairs or down, no sound of computer or TV. If Bia *hadn't* left with Lynette, he was being unusually quiet. Was he spying on me, or hoping to catch me by surprise? I had to get out of here fast.

I hurried to the bathroom and turned on the light for a quick look at my hair. It was a mess. I grabbed the brush. But I couldn't seem to make my hair look right. Was it because my hand was so shaky? Why was I wasting my time like this? I was only going to see Dominic. I threw down the brush. And then I suddenly leaned forward, staring into the mirror.

The pimple on my chin had returned. And there was another one on my nose.

I felt cold. Why wasn't my skin perfect anymore? Why had Mark been so abrupt? I became aware of a queasiness in my stomach. Maybe I really *didn't* feel so hot.

"Don't be stupid. It's just coincidence," I said. My voice sounded hollow. The phone rang, and I jumped.

I raced to answer it, flooded with relief. It had to be Mark, apologizing, telling me he'd give me a ride after all. Everything was okay, not ominous at all. Nothing had changed. I lifted the receiver. It was Gloria.

"I just *had* to tell you!" she shouted. No laryngitis now! "I peeled the mask off—and it *worked!* My skin looks a million times better. Lynette will *die* when she sees me."

I didn't bother telling her that by tomorrow Lynette's skin would look just as good as hers. I couldn't think of anything to say.

"Well, Julie? You still there?"

I mumbled something about how happy I was to hear her good news.

"You don't *sound* happy," she said. "You know something, Julie . . ." She paused. "Well, I think I should tell you. You've been kind of full of yourself lately, I was noticing."

"I have to go, I don't feel so hot." It wasn't a lie. I put down the receiver.

The pattern was very clear.

13

I stood there by the phone, feeling the sickness in my stomach. I pushed my hair back from my forehead. My hand was damp with sweat.

The transition had been so sudden! All at once the spirit was against me. What had changed her from my protector to my enemy? It had to be something that had happened after I came home—everyone had treated me like a princess at school today.

And then I remembered how long Bia and Lynette waited before driving away. Was it because I accused him of not being the real Thamrongsak? As soon as he knew I'd figured out the truth he must have done something. He could have told Lynette to wait for him, and then given the spirit one more gift—maybe something precious he was saving for an emergency, something that had finally won her over. *That* was why it had taken them so long to leave. And that was why the spirit was out to get me now. When she'd been against Bia, she punished his friends. Now that she was with him, she was punishing me, his enemy.

I felt like I was going to throw up, or faint, or both. I squeezed my eyes shut, breathing deeply, trying not to panic.

I had to get to the junior high and find Dominic, and he would help me. I could tell him everything, I could trust him, he would know what to do. He was the only person in the world who wouldn't think I was crazy. He had built the spirit house, after all. He'd be *thrilled* to learn how well it worked. Good old Dom!

And then I moaned. What if Bia got to him first? Bia knew Dominic was the only person I could turn to. Bia knew where he was. Bia had Lynette to drive him around. He could probably come up with reasons to keep Dominic from believing my story. And just by being there, Bia would prevent me from confiding in Dominic, from telling him the truth.

I wouldn't let him stop me. Bia already knew I had figured him out. I would just have to tell Dominic, right in front of him. It wouldn't be easy. But it was the only thing I could do.

That wasn't true. It wasn't the *only* thing. There was something else I could do first, one more precaution I could take.

I looked down at my wrist, at the bracelet Mark had given me. There was still a chance I could stack the cards, at least partially, in my favor again. The bracelet might get the spirit back on my side. Then she'd protect me, make me safe; she'd fix my skin and hair and make everyone like me again. I started for the backyard. I ran past Mom's study. . . .

"No. Not for you!"

My own voice stopped me in the hallway. I leaned

against the wall, breathing heavily. I was so scared and confused I was talking to myself now. But so what? The advice I was giving was good.

It didn't work to make wishes for yourself. I'd realized that weeks ago, when I made my first deal with the spirit. And passing Mom's study now, the right wish had popped into my head out of nowhere, just as if someone else really *had* suggested it. It seemed absolutely self-evident. It was what I should have wished for in the first place. It was really the only wish to make.

I felt a sudden calm, a clarity, a deep warmth rising from inside me. I knew what to ask for. It might not make me safe. But it would do something more important. It would make things right.

I tried to keep up the feeling of calm as I stepped out into the darkening backyard. There was not a break in the clouds; dead leaves danced across the lawn and blew into my face. And as I neared the spirit house I began to notice a thick rotten smell. A smell that made me think of cramped animal cages needing to be cleaned—a smell of illness and filth.

Was it the odor of the spirit? A stench she was giving off because she was becoming more active, more powerful? Or did it just smell this way to me now because she was my enemy?

I stopped beside the spirit house, feeling queasier than ever. I couldn't take this stink for very long. But the wish was short—and final. I'd do it and stay away from the spirit house for good.

I got down on my knees, as I had seen Bia doing, put my hands on the ground in front of me, and rested my head on them.

I offer you my most respectful greetings, honorable one.
This is Julie Kamen again. Please accept my gratitude for
all the help you have given to me. It is very much
appreciated. But there is one more request I must make.
It is very important. For this, I offer you the most valuable
possession I have left.

What I ask you is to please let Thamrongsak Tan-
ngarmtrong come to America. Let him take his rightful
place here. Please do this. It is my deepest and most sincere
wish. I offer you my humblest gratitude for listening to
me. Thank you.

I got to my feet, trying not to think of the spirit's
face, of her head lolling on its pillow of intestines. That's
what I was smelling, the foulness of her intestines. It
was all I could do not to gag as I stepped closer. I
gritted my teeth and thrust my hand through the little
doorway. I dropped Mark's bracelet inside.

My fingers touched something pulpy and moist and
very warm.

I screamed and pulled my hand out and turned to run.
And screamed again when Bia grabbed me.

14

"Quiet. Quiet, Julie. Quiet, please. What is *matter?*"

"Let go of me!" I howled. I struggled against him, grasping his wrists, trying to push his hands away from my shoulders. I was too hysterical to think; I hardly knew what I was saying. "Let me go! You can't make her hurt me like you made her hurt Thamrongsak!"

"Quiet, Julie! Somebody hear."

"I'll scream again if you don't let go!"

He dropped his hands but didn't step back; he'd grab me again if I tried to get away. His hair was rumpled, his black and white shirt untucked. "What *happen?*" he whispered.

I knew I had to get away from him but I couldn't run; my knees were so weak I could barely stand. "Oh, God, I *touched* her, I *felt* her." I gulped, shivering with disgust. "She was in there. I felt her. All slimy and warm and . . . *horrible.*"

"Spirit? You feel spirit?" he asked me, puzzled.

"What *else?*"

And then, unbelievably, he laughed. "Oh, Julie!" He threw back his head, his shoulders shaking. "You think is spirit, when you touch the . . . the . . ." He couldn't go on.

"Well, what *was* it then?" I demanded.

He took a deep breath, trying to control his amusement. "Boil . . . boil pig brain," he said.

"What?" The words had no meaning for me. "What are you saying? I don't get it."

"Boil pig brain," he repeated, wiping his eyes. "Buy it when shop for Thai meal other day. Special food. Spirit like very much. Today, warm in microwave. Then give to spirit."

"Boiled *pig's* brain?" It was too ridiculous to be possible. That was the special gift he had given the spirit? *That* was how he had wooed her onto his side? "Come on, Bia! You've got to be kidding."

"No. Is true. Old custom," he explained, serious now, still very close to me.

"That's great," I muttered. "I hope she thinks it's delicious." I felt stupid for being so hysterical, and angry at him for laughing at me. But my knees weren't shaking anymore; I was beginning to pull myself together. The situation was coming back to me. I didn't know whether the bracelet would have any effect or not—it was probably a paltry gift compared with a boiled pig's brain.

But I was sure that in a minute Bia would do something. He would try to keep me quiet, to stop me from getting away from him and telling anybody what I knew. I looked at my watch. It was only four-fifteen. Nobody else would be home for at least an hour. That would give Bia plenty of time. Unless I could get to Dominic.

Thunder rumbled distantly; the wind lifted my hair. "So you *were* here all this time," I said, stalling. "I thought you were out with Lynette."

"Talk to her. Then come back and start to cut vegetable for supper." He looked down at the ground, pushing leaves aside with his foot.

He didn't explain why he had come back in so quietly that I didn't hear him, or why he had made no noise at all inside the house. But I didn't accuse him of trying to make me think he wasn't there; I didn't want to do anything to make him angry. I just wanted to get to Dominic. "That was nice of you. To start supper, I mean."

"Ah, there, I see." He knelt and picked up something from the dead leaves, something he must have dropped when I ran into him.

It was a large chef's knife.

He lifted the knife and carefully brushed off the blade. His eyes moved back to me. He was standing straight now, I noticed. There were no dark circles under his eyes. He looked better than he had in weeks. "What you give spirit this time?" he said softly.

I had to get away from him. "None of your business," I said. I stepped backward. Would he try to stab me if I ran for it? I turned and started walking slowly across the lawn, pushing dead leaves out of my hair.

He kept beside me. "Where you going?"

I didn't look at him. "None of your business."

"No. I think is my business, Julie." His tone was chilling because it was so bland, so pleasant. "Don't want you to talk to anybody now. Want you to stay with me, help me. Explain what you say about Thamrongsak." He reached for my arm. "What you—"

"Bia, *look!*" I shouted, pointing to the left.

It was the oldest trick in the book, but he fell for it. He turned and stared back in the direction of the spirit house.

I took off. I ran past the deck, around the side of the house toward the front.

"No, Julie!" he shouted.

I had a slight head start, but he was after me now. I didn't look behind; I kept going. I raced across the front yard.

"Stop, Julie! Want to explain!"

Sure you do, I thought. *You want to explain that I'm about to have a very bad accident with a knife, because I know too much. You want to explain that the spirit didn't get me yet, so you will.*

I reached the sidewalk and pounded down the block. I heard his footsteps slapping the pavement close behind me as the first drops of rain started to fall. I reached the corner. I dashed into the street.

Tires squealed as a Mercedes swerved. The horn blared; the driver was yelling. My heart thudded wildly, pumping more adrenaline through me as I reached the curb. An accident! The spirit *was* trying to stop me. I wanted to be at home, safe in my room, not plunging into danger. I kept going. I wouldn't be safe at home. I wouldn't be safe anywhere with Bia.

I didn't hear his steps now. I looked back for a second. Bia was still on the other side of the street, trapped there by the traffic.

I turned and kept running. Maybe I *could* make it to the junior high before he did. I wasn't as fast as most boys. But Bia smoked. He'd be winded first. He wouldn't be able to keep up the pace for long. And he didn't know the streets. People drove him everywhere he went. If I could lose him, it might take him hours to find his way back home. That would give me time to tell enough people about him to be safe. I darted abruptly to the left, around a corner. I ran halfway down the block, then slowed a little and looked back.

He was around the corner too, gaining on me. I turned and slammed into a fat man. His umbrella clattered to the ground.

"Look where you're going!" he shouted at me.

"Sorry," I said, and stumbled into his umbrella. The point at the top jabbed me painfully in the leg. If Bia's knife didn't get me, the spirit would. I pushed the umbrella aside and kept going. *The bracelet! I gave you the bracelet!* I thought at the spirit.

But that wouldn't help me. I hadn't given her the bracelet so she would protect me. I gave it to her so she'd bring Thamrongsak to America. I had to watch out for her tricks and look where I was going. I dodged out of the way of an old lady and a dog—and skidded and almost fell. The sidewalk was very slippery now.

Reflected lightning rippled across the wet black pavement, followed instantly by a tremendous boom of thunder. Next time it might hit me. Or it would hit a tree I was under and a branch would fall on me. I was out of breath; my chest ached. And still I heard Bia's steps behind me. Why wasn't he out of breath yet? Was the spirit giving him extra wind? I splashed through a puddle and turned another corner, gasping.

I wasn't far from the junior high now. But Bia was still following me. How was I going to lose him? I reached a narrow street that curved away to the left, the wrong direction. If I ran down it would I throw him off? It might be easier to lose him there; the streets down that way twisted and turned. And after I lost him I could work my way back, and find Dominic, and . . .

But those streets were dark, and empty of people. They would be the perfect place for Bia to get me. I couldn't risk it. I turned right at the next corner.

There was the junior high, three blocks straight ahead, at the top of the hill. If I didn't do something he'd see me go inside. I turned right at the next corner. By going one block out of the way, and then turning back at the corner just before the school, I might be out of his sight long enough to get into the building without being seen.

I was really hurting now, going much slower than when I had started. My clammy dress clung to my skin, my shoes squelched with every step. Rain poured down. I hugged my arms to my sides, pushing up the hill, teeth chattering uncontrollably. My lips were salty from my runny nose.

At the last intersection I looked back. Bia was almost a block behind me. I turned left and dashed for the school, sobbing for breath. If *only* I could get inside before Bia reached the corner and saw me!

The spirit sent branches skittering along the sidewalk to slow me down. I kicked them away, my eyes fixed on the steps and the double doors. Two large trees bent and swayed on either side of the school entrance, limbs creaking. I knew the spirit was going to fling a heavy branch down on my head when I ran underneath those trees. But I had to risk it; there was no other way to get in.

I bent over, my arms covering my head, and ran for the doors. I was sure I heard the crack of a limb tearing loose. But I was at the doors. I couldn't look behind to find out if Bia had rounded the corner and could see where I was going, I didn't have one second to spare. I pulled open the door and staggered inside.

Into darkness.

The door slammed, echoed, faded to silence. I had been too busy to notice from outside that there were no lights in the windows. But now it was clear that the power at the school was out.

I sank back against a wall, my throat catching, tears rolling down my wet face. No wonder the spirit had allowed me to get all the way to the school! Dominic wouldn't be here to help me if the power was out. The building would be almost empty. And it was so dark. How perfect for Bia! He must have seen me going in. He was probably running up the steps right this minute. With his knife.

I lurched away from the wall, through the entrance hallway, and into the main corridor. All I could see were the vague gray patches of the classroom doors on either side. I had to get help before Bia found me. But was anybody even here to help me? Maybe the custodian. And the custodian would be in the basement, where his office must be, and all the electrical stuff. It would be even darker down there.

But I didn't have any choice. There was probably a stairway at the end of the hall. I moved slowly to the right, feeling my way with one hand against the wall. My footsteps on the linoleum reverberated along the length of the corridor.

Behind me the front door slammed shut with clanging finality. When its echoes died, I heard footsteps quickly approaching.

15

Maybe I could hide from him in a classroom. After he went past it, I could sneak back through the corridor and get out the front doors. I groped my way forward. I grasped a doorknob and turned and pushed, hoping it wouldn't make much noise. The door opened silently. I stepped quietly through.

And fell, crying out, my arms stretched in front of me. My shin hit the edge of something, my ankle twisted, my arms and upper body slammed into a sharp metal object that crashed resoundingly to the floor. I lay there whimpering, holding on to my ankle, which throbbed with hot pain.

The spirit had really done it now, sending me blindly into what must be the orchestra room, a series of tiers. I had stumbled over the first step, wrenching my ankle, knocking over a music stand. My ankle hurt too much for me even to stand up, let alone run. I dragged myself forward.

The door clicked open. Bia didn't know about the

orchestra room. But he had heard me fall, he was prepared for obstacles. He stepped carefully down. "Julie?" he whispered. And then he was crouching on the floor beside me.

I started to scream for help. But before even the first syllable came out Bia's hand was clamped over my mouth. I struggled, grunting. His hand tightened.

"Listen to me!" he whispered, panting harshly.

Maybe he wasn't going to kill me instantly. He wanted to tell me something. If I kept trying to scream he'd have to shut me up. But if I was quiet, he might talk for a while. Maybe long enough for the custodian to come and investigate the noise. Maybe long enough for me to convince Bia not to hurt me.

The pressure of his hand relaxed. "No screaming?" he asked me.

"No," I whispered, shaking my head on the floor.

He lifted his hand, but kept it an inch from my mouth just to make sure. "Good."

I pushed myself up into a sitting position, trying not to move my ankle. "What . . . what did you want to tell me?"

"How you find out I'm not Thamrongsak?"

If only I hadn't told him that! But maybe I could still make him believe I didn't know enough to be dangerous to him. "I don't know why I said that. It just . . . popped into my head. But I don't have any *proof* or anything. Nobody else would believe me."

"You don't tell anybody?"

"No. I didn't. I promise."

"Good." He sighed and shifted on his knees beside me. "I think spirit not so angry now—so okay for me to tell you. And maybe you can help me. Can't tell you before, ask you for help, because not safe."

I wasn't sure what he meant. Had the spirit prevented him from telling me the truth before? Why would she do that? But I didn't want to doubt or question him. I had to humor him. "I'll help you, I promise," I said. "Go on. Tell me."

"Not easy . . ."

Was this going to be the truth, or just more lies to make him look good? In either case, it might clarify some things—and put off whatever he was going to do to me. "Tell me, Bia. I won't tell anybody, believe me."

"Then why you run away?"

What could I say? He had reason to be suspicious. Maybe a little bit of truth from me might convince him to trust me. "I was looking for Dominic. This is his school. I just wanted to ask him . . . if you told him anything."

"For sure? That all?"

Scared as I was, I was getting a little impatient. He had dangled some tempting revelation in front of me, and now he was pulling it back. "Why else would I come here? I didn't run to Mom and Dad. I didn't call the high school, or any of my friends. Trust me, Bia. Who is Thamrongsak? How do you know him?"

"Well . . ." He cleared his throat, and then coughed. "Sak—Thamrongsak nickname—his mother cousin of my mother. Good boy, work all the time. His family neighbor of my parent in Chon Buri. Very poor family, like my parent." He stopped.

"Go on, Bia," I said.

"Well . . . Don't visit parent for long, long time. Then,

_111_

go to see them, my mother tell me Sak, he going to America. In three day he going! Rich American family pay for him, change his future forever. And I think about my future."

Was this the truth? It might be. It made sense that Thamrongsak was a relative of Bia's; that explained the similarity in their appearance. I heard the rustle of Bia's hand in his shirt pocket.

"Go ahead and smoke," I told him.

"Is okay? Smoke in school?"

He chased me here with a knife and then worries about smoking? "No. But it doesn't matter now." I wanted Bia to relax, lower his guard, open up. And the odor of smoke, it occurred to me, might help the custodian find us.

He lit up and inhaled deeply, with obvious relief. "You were saying about your future," I prompted him.

"Have very bad job in Bangkok, no future." His voice was dull. "I am very much hopeless. Then, I hear about Sak going to America. And I think maybe something like that can happen to me, make me not so hopeless for future. So, I go home from parent, and stop at Erewan Shrine. Very holy place. Everybody know spirit there very powerful. Always many flower at shrine, from people who spirit help them, many people praying, and they put leaf gold on elephant statue, to thank spirit. So I ask spirit . . ." His voice faded. He inhaled deeply again.

"What did you ask the spirit?"

My eyes were adjusting to the darkness. In the dim light from the windows I could see that he was looking directly at me now, the burning cigarette forgotten in his hand. "I ask spirit—please make me going to America, like Sak."

Sure, I felt like saying. It was easy enough for him to tell me his wish had been innocent. But I kept my mouth shut. If I doubted him, he might stop. And even now, there was a part of me that wanted to believe him.

"I ask that, and I promise to give spirit Buddha pendant before I am go to America. Pendant very holy, very, very valuable."

"The friend who gave it to you must have a lot of money then."

"Chai, old friend from childhood. Many time he do thing to make money, not very good thing, maybe illegal. Then he like to spend money. Give me gift, pendant, lighter. So, I make promise to give pendant to spirit if help me go to America. And then . . ."

He bent his head. Suddenly I was afraid of what was coming.

". . . after three day, go again to Chon Buri, to party for Sak on morning of day he leave to America. But is no people, no party. And my father tell me . . ." He paused again, and then went on quickly. "Very bad accident. Big truck, hit Sak. Happen only few hour after I pray to spirit. Sak in hospital, like dead, except only breathing. Doctor say Sak, he never get better. My father say I must go to hospital. And in hospital, Sak father ask me to help him."

He swallowed. "Sak father want to stay at hospital. He ask me to mail airline ticket back to family in America, special way with insurance. He give me ticket, immigration paper, I-20 form, ask me to write note in English explaining for American family about accident.

Then I know. I know for sure what make accident happen. I am very unhappy, very afraid."

His face seemed as impassive as ever, but his voice had become hoarse, unsteady. I wanted so much to believe that he hadn't wished the accident on Thamrongsak!

But Bia had chased me with a knife; Bia was an actor and a liar. And what was to stop him from lying about this? There was no way I could ever find out what he had really wished.

"On bus I read ticket. Plane is leaving only few hour. What am I do? Spirit put ticket *in my hand*. Will not make Sak well again if I do not use ticket. Will be only . . . only waste of ticket.

"So, I am in big hurry, only few hour. I find my friend Chai. Tell him everything. He help me. I can send letter and money from America to Chai, for my parent. He mail to them from Bangkok, so nobody know I am in America. Many time I do not visit parent for many month, only send letter and money. Chai lend me clothes for America, lend me money, lend me bag, pay taxi to airport. I get on plane."

"Wait a minute," I said. "You were using Sak's ticket, with his name on it. But your passport has *your* name on it. Didn't they notice?"

"I am lucky; many tourist in airport, crowded, late, hurrying. Man at check-in very busy, look only at ticket, tell me to hurry to passport control. Man at passport control look at passport quick, do not check name in English on ticket. Think maybe I'm safe, no more problem. Get on plane. Very excited now—America! Plane take off. And lady in next seat say to me, 'Oh, what beautiful jade Buddha pendant!' "

"So *that's* it," I said, putting my hand to my mouth.

"Am so hurry, forget to pay spirit!" Bia said, shaking his head, as though he himself were still shocked by it. "First, very scared! Afraid plane fall down! But then I think: in America, do not have Thai spirit, do not have spirit house. In America, I am safe from spirit." He pulled out another cigarette.

"And in America," I murmured, "Dominic builds you a Thai spirit house."

"Yes." Bia nodded, blowing out smoke. "Thank you very much, Dominic."

"What happened next?" I said. "The phone call. What was—"

"Wait. Not yet. First, before Dominic make spirit house, I give you Buddha pendant," he said. "I give because you help me, you such a good friend. And because I like you very much."

I wished he hadn't said that. Lying to me now only detracted from his credibility. How could he expect me to believe he liked me after the way he had treated me—ignoring me, going out with Gloria and Lynette?

"I give you Buddha pendant because I like you, and because I think I am safe from spirit now. And then Dominic give me spirit house—spirit house he start to make on Saturday. And in next minute is phone call—from my friend Chai."

"I was right! It was a friend of yours. That's why he asked for Thamrongsak, not Bia," I burst out.

"Sure. He want you to think I'm Thamrongsak," Bia said. "And he tell me—Sak get well. Is miracle! I don't have phone, so my mother sometime phone to Chai to give big news to me. She say, Sak right away write letter to family in America, saying he want to come now, please send back ticket. Happen because I do not pay spirit, give Buddha pendant to you. Spirit my enemy, punish me now, make bad for me, good for Sak."

He paused, and then said lightly, "Bad for me, and bad also for my friend—especially bad for girl friend. That how spirit work." He carefully put his cigarette out on the floor.

I went cold, then hot again. Was it possible? All along Bia had been going out with Gloria and Lynette to protect *me*?

It had worked, hadn't it? Just telling me I was boring hadn't convinced the spirit, so Bia went further. As soon as he told the spirit I was his enemy, Mark called and everything started going well for me—and bad for Gloria and Lynette. The logic was flawless. And if that meant he really *did* like me, then maybe I could relax now. Maybe I didn't have to worry that he would hurt me. It all made sense.

Except, I saw, for one or two things. I reminded myself that he could still be lying about his motivation. "But why didn't you just ask me for the pendant back? Wouldn't that have satisfied the spirit and prevented a whole lot of trouble?"

"Don't want to ask for pendant. Want you to have. Also, not good to give holy thing, then take back."

I should have known better than to believe him! I was too angry and disappointed to watch what I was saying. "Sure. You wanted me to have the pendant. And then, when I put the pendant in the spirit house, you just left it there. And it disappeared because the spirit took it." I sighed, shaking my head. "You expect me to believe that—now that I *know* how important the pendant is to you?"

"No," Bia said quietly. "Spirit not take pendant. I take."

"What?" I could hardly believe he was admitting it.

"I take Buddha pendant from spirit house, I keep in room, saving to give to spirit. I lie to you about it. I'm sorry. I lie, because do not want to tell you about me, when spirit so angry at me. Not safe for you."

"But . . ." I tried to think clearly, to figure it all out. At least he wasn't lying about taking the pendant. Did that mean the rest of his story was the truth?

The spirit wasn't angry at him anymore. I knew that because of how she had turned against me this afternoon. That must mean he'd given her the pendant this afternoon. I hadn't felt it in there today, but it could have been covered by the pig's brain. "But I put the pendant in there weeks ago. You took it out weeks ago. Why did you wait until *today* to give it to her?" I asked him.

He stood up and took a few steps away from me. "First, try giving lighter, other precious thing I have. Spirit still angry. Then today you say I not the real Thamrongsak. So I think you know something. Now time for telling you truth. So I give pig brain to spirit. And also give pendant. Spirit not so angry now. That mean safe to be friend with you again. Tell you truth. Ask for help from you."

I wasn't satisfied. There were too many holes. If he'd known all along that the pendant would placate the spirit, he wouldn't have gone on living under a cloud all those weeks. He would have given it to her right away.

But I didn't question him about it again; I wanted him to think I believed him so he'd trust me, and we could get out of here. "So . . . what kind of help do you want from me now?" I asked him.

"Please, Julie." He quickly sat down beside me again. "Help me . . . hide letter." He sounded almost humble. "Letter from Sak. And help me know what to say to your parent."

"What letter? The one your friend told you about? Sak must have mailed it a month ago."

"No, not that one. Already take that, burn it. Another letter . . . about Sak coming to America."

"What are you talking about?"

"Sak better now. Coming to America."

"*What?*"

"Yes. Very good news. But want you to help me hide letter, so parent do not see. Help me know what to tell parent. Very important, nobody say anything to Sak about me."

"But Sak doesn't have a *ticket*, Bia!" I said, exasperated. "You took it. Remember?"

"Oh. Forget to say. Somebody give him another ticket. Chai write and tell me. Sak coming now. Don't want him to know about me. Don't want his parent or my parent to know what happen."

I shook my head, baffled. So much of his story *did* ring true. I had almost been able to believe that his innocent wish had backfired, that the ticket had been handed to him, and he had forgotten to pay the spirit in Thailand. It made sense of so much that had happened. Even the timing was right, in relation to the spirit house and the phone call and everything else.

But I couldn't ignore the two major flaws in his story. Why had he waited so long before giving the pendant to the spirit? And how had Sak gotten another ticket?

And then I noticed that both of his hands were free. They had been all along. "Where's the knife, Bia?" I asked him.

"Knife?"

"The knife you were holding, in the backyard."

He shrugged, as if it didn't matter. "Must be I drop in garden."

I almost laughed. He *hadn't* been chasing me with it! That, at least, was a relief. "Maybe . . . maybe we should go home now," I said.

"Hope you do not tell parent. I tell you truth about what I ask spirit. Am very happy Sak coming. But don't want Sak to find out about me."

"All right. I won't tell them right away." I still didn't believe Sak was coming. "I'll think about it. Can you help me up?"

He stood up and pulled me to my feet. My ankle had stopped hurting. I wasn't sure what that meant, in relation to the spirit. And suddenly I was just too tired and bewildered to try to figure it out.

"You believe me, Julie?"

"I want to," I said.

We walked slowly. The rain had stopped now. On the way, he asked me again if I would help him check the mail so we could find and hide the letter before anyone else saw it. I told him that I would.

But by the time we got home, they had already read the letter.

16

"Where have you been?" Mom said when I appeared, wet and bedraggled, in the kitchen doorway.

Mom and Dad and Dominic were sitting at the table. Dominic had his hand on a large gray envelope with foreign stamps on it. It had been torn open. I moved toward it.

"Julie! You're getting mud all over the clean floor," Mom said. "Can't you think for once? Maybe you need to go to Thailand and learn how to take your shoes off in the house."

Things were back to normal. I wasn't Miss Perfection anymore. I had kind of gotten used to it. But at least the spirit didn't seem to be my enemy either—she hadn't left me with a sprained ankle.

"Is Bia with you?" Dominic said eagerly, lifting the envelope. "He . . . he better read this."

"He went right upstairs. I don't think he . . . I mean . . ."

"Get him down," Dad said. "This is important."

I left my shoes in my room and knocked on Bia's door.

"Yes?" he said from inside.

"They have a letter," I said against the door. "They want you to come down and read it."

The door swung open. "Letter?" Bia said urgently. "They get already?"

"I think so. It looks like it's from Thailand."

He stiffened. "But they . . . must not see."

"It's too late, Bia. They've read it."

His eyes darkened. He looked quickly back into his room, as though he wished he could hide there. But only a moment later his face went blank. He squared his shoulders and came with me down the stairs. I couldn't help being impressed by the composure with which he was approaching this confrontation that I knew he dreaded.

I was dying of curiosity, of course. "Please come and read this letter, Bia," Dad said in the kitchen. "We need an explanation."

"But how did it get here?" I asked them. "It wasn't in the mail today."

"I picked it up at the post office," Dominic said. "Nobody was here when I came home—but there was this notice, attempt to deliver a package, from Thailand. Certified, Express Mail. I was curious. And it was just addressed to the Kamen family, so I thought they might let me pick it up. They wouldn't have, if I didn't have my photo ID with our address. But they finally gave it to me."

I was aware, as Bia and I bent over the letter, of what my first wish had been: that Dominic should discover the truth about Bia.

To my dear family, the Kamens,

How are you? I hope you are well. I am so happy to meet you soon!

Thank you, thank you! I was so afraid you forgot about me. I was afraid you do not get the ticket my parents sent back to you. So, I am very happy when I receive the envelope from America with your return address on it and the international money order inside! Now I know you do not forget, and you are happy to hear the news about my miracle recovery from car accident, surely the work of prayer and the Lord Buddha.

Perhaps you do not write a letter because you are very busy I can understand this. What you do instead is important thing—to send me the money for a new ticket, as I asked in my letter, so I can come to America after all. Thank you very very much for your great kindness to me.

I have reservation on Asia Airways, flight 72, arriving at 16 o'clock on 20 October. Can you please send me telegram wire to confirm you know of my arrival, and are meeting me?

Thank you again very very much with all my heart, and from my parents and grandparents also. You are kind and wonderful people. My happiness is so great I can't express.

From your new son, with all my heart,

Thamrongsak Tan-ngarmtrong
"Sak"

The spirit had granted both my wishes.

But why had it taken so long for my first request to be answered, when I had made it weeks ago? Had she waited until I had given her the bracelet because the pendant didn't count, since it had already been pledged to her? I didn't know.

But I did think I knew why the end of Bia's story—as he had told it to me—hadn't made sense. The answer I'd gotten from the letter seemed almost too good to be true.

But what other explanation was there? Bia was the only person here who knew what had happened to Sak. No one else could have sent him the money—from America, with our address on the envelope. And I had thought there could be no actual proof of what Bia's wish really had been! Now, here it was.

The fact that Bia had tried to hide what he had done only made it more believable. Not to mention, Dominic had discovered the letter. That meant it contained the truth about Bia.

"Okay, Bia," Mom said. "Who sent this person the money? Who *is* he, anyway?"

"I need to talk to Bia for a minute," I said, before he had a chance to answer.

"That's not *fair!*" Dominic wailed. "We deserve to know what's going on. Don't we?"

"You're darn right we do," Mom said. "Spill it, Bia. And Julie, you just keep out of it."

"Just let us—"

The phone rang. Maybe we had a chance. The spirit made good use of phone calls.

Dad answered it. "Oh, hi, Sam," he said. Sam was his boss at the newspaper. "Listen, could I call you back in . . . *What?* You're kidding! When?" He looked at his watch, then grabbed the pad by the phone and started scribbling.

"What's the matter? What happened?" Mom was asking him.

"Come on, Bia." I pulled him out of the kitchen.

Dominic trotted after us. "I'm coming too. I deserve to know what's going on."

"Fine, Dom." It didn't matter if Dominic heard us. "The pendant, the lighter, the other precious things," I asked Bia, steering him through the living room. "Where did you sell them?"

"What?" Bia stopped, staring at me.

"That's how you got the money for Sak's ticket, isn't it?"

He didn't answer.

"Sak got the money from America—in an envelope with our address on it," I reminded him.

"I sell thing to shop," he said slowly. "Pawnshop, I think is word. Downtown. Lynette drive me."

"I *knew* what you said today didn't make sense—about hanging on to the pendant all this time before giving it to the spirit. About Sak getting another ticket, out of nowhere."

"What are you talking about?" Dominic begged us.

"Hold on, Dominic. We'll tell you." I thought of something. "Wait a minute, Bia. Couldn't you have just sent him the original ticket? Or sold that one to get the money?"

"Ticket only for America to Thailand—not work other way. And I can't sell. Person who buy ticket only can sell. I ask. Anyway, it no refund ticket."

That was also true.

"And," Bia added, "not my ticket to sell. Belong to family. Only make worse, if sell that."

The ticket was the proof of what Bia had asked the

spirit. If he had wished an accident on Sak, then he wouldn't have sent him money—ruining his *own* chances here. He would have burned the first letter and forgotten it, telling no one, ignoring Sak's request for another ticket. He probably could have gotten away with it. With no response, Sak would have given up and stopped writing. This letter was solid evidence that Bia meant no harm to Sak, that his wish had been innocent.

"Why didn't you tell me, Bia? Today, when you told me everything else, you should have told me about sending Sak the money for the ticket. It explains everything."

"Not tell because that my problem to solve, not yours." And I knew, from his tone of voice, that he wouldn't say anything else about it. This was one area that he would not share with me.

He had done a genuinely noble thing, and yet he had tried to hide it from everybody. It was similar to the way he had pretended to dislike me in order to protect me from the spirit. I couldn't imagine Mark doing that; I also couldn't imagine Mark selling everything he had to send a distant relative the money for a ticket.

Until now, I hadn't imagined there was this side to Bia. I had thought his reserved manner was hiding something sinister, when in fact it was exactly the reverse. And now that I was beginning to understand what he was really like, my feelings for him were radically changing. I had never felt such admiration for anybody. Suddenly I was determined that, no matter what happened, I was going to keep on knowing him. I wouldn't let him slip out of my life.

I squeezed Bia's arm, tugging him out onto the deck. "Everything's going to be fine," I told him. "Believe me."

"I don't think so." He looked around the dark yard. "Where you taking me?"

"I have one more thing to ask the spirit, one more wish." I didn't know if Thai wishes went in threes, but most other kinds did.

He resisted a little as we neared the spirit house. "Have to understand, Julie. Spirit not so angry at me today, because I give pig brain. But . . ."

"But what?"

"But not enough. Spirit never really forgive me. I never really be safe—until give spirit Buddha pendant. Because that what I promise. Soon, spirit angry at me again."

That was something I hadn't realized. It only made me more impressed that Bia had given me the pendant in the first place, and then sacrificed it for Sak.

"But the spirit granted my wishes. Both of them," I said. "Look, I've got a plan. Take me to the shop where you sold the Buddha pendant. I'll make a deposit, I'll buy it back someday. And then I'll give it back to the spirit"—I took a deep breath—"when I'm in Thailand."

"You? In Thailand?" Bia stared at me, his mouth open. For once I had really floored him.

"I'll go there. The spirit gave me everything else I wished for. Why shouldn't she bring me to Thailand too? Especially if I promise to give her the pendant there. That's what started the whole thing. That's what she really wants. That will solve your problems with her. Not to mention, *I'll* have a *really* unusual vacation."

He smiled at me, an open, natural smile, as though he was finally beginning to believe things might be okay after all. "A vacation in Thailand you never forget, Julie," he said, his voice full of warmth. "I promise you that."

126

17

There is a two-note chime as the seat-belt light blinks on. The cabin attendant makes the announcement in Japanese, Thai, and English: "Please fasten your seat belt, and make sure your seat back and tray table are locked in the upright position for our arrival in Bangkok."

I've been flying for twenty-four hours, awake most of the time. I was so dazed and exhausted when I changed planes in Tokyo that I almost missed the connection. But now my fatigue has melted away like the old makeup I washed off in the bathroom a few minutes ago. I'm bursting with energy and impatience as I peer out the window at the green and brown landscape, the tiny red-roofed buildings. In ten minutes I'll be in Thailand. And I'll see Bia again! It's amazing how much I've missed him.

Though I have to admit I did enjoy having Sak around. He was very different from Bia in some ways, very proper and studious. There was less mystery to him, partly because he wasn't living a lie and partly just because his English was so much better. But there were similarities too—his rare but irresistible smile, his quiet voice, his beautiful manners, his respect for Mom and Dad and the teachers. And once he got over his initial shyness, he surprised us all with a crazy sense of humor. He was always finding something to laugh with us about. I learned a little Thai from him. I can't wait until Bia hears me!

Bia ended up telling Mom and Dad the truth, at my urging. Of course they didn't think the spirit had done anything—*that* was nothing but coincidence! It was true that nothing really impossible had happened. And it actually worked to Bia's advantage that Mom and Dad didn't believe in the spirit. It freed him from any responsibility for Sak's accident, in their eyes. They just thought the ticket had accidentally fallen into his hands and he had rashly used it, believing that Sak couldn't. They were so impressed by what Bia had done to get Sak the money that they forgave him for pretending to be someone he wasn't. Most important of all, they understood why Sak, and his family, must never know who Bia really was.

But there was no way we could pretend to Sak that another Thai boy hadn't been living with us. Even if everyone in the family could have managed to keep Bia's presence a secret—which was doubtful—the other kids and the teachers would certainly have mentioned him to Sak.

The story we told everyone wasn't too distant from the truth: the boy named Bia had taken advantage of Sak's accident and come in his place under his name. But when Sak got well, we said, Bia insisted on going back, out of fairness to the boy we originally intended to sponsor. The school administrators were a little puzzled at first, but all it took was Sak's passport to prove to them that this boy really was Thamrongsak Tan-ngarm-trong, and soon they accepted the situation.

Sak was the most surprised by the story, and we gave him a few more details. We said Bia confessed to us that he had stolen Sak's ticket and papers from the post office in Bangkok, where he worked at night cleaning the floors. "So strange, so strange," Sak kept saying, shaking his head.

It was fortunate that no one photographed Bia while he was with us, or Sak would certainly have recognized him. But what was most important was that Bia had taken the extra precaution of giving us a false nickname. He didn't know he was going to do it, he said, until he arrived—and then the name *Bia* just popped into his head. His parents, and Sak's parents, will never suspect he used Sak's ticket to come to America. It was a *kamoi,* a thief named Bia, who stole the ticket from the post office—not Kob, who they believed faithfully mailed it.

I'm the only one in our family who knows Bia's real name is Kob. I'm the only one who knows his address in Bangkok. He and I have been writing to each other, but I haven't shown anyone else his letters. And though I've been writing to him as Kob for eight months, I still think of him as Bia.

I studied harder than I ever had before, and I did so well in school that Mom and Dad are rewarding me by giving me a trip to Thailand for the summer. I didn't tell them that was the third wish I made.

And because they're paying for the trip, I was able to buy back the Buddha pendant from the pawnshop with my savings and extra money I earned from baby-sitting and working part-time at the library. I kept going back to check on it, making a payment each time. And luckily, no one else wanted it that whole time. Yesterday I made the final payment, and put it around my neck again. And tomorrow I'll give it to the spirit, as I promised her I would, at the Erewan Shrine, where Bia made his first bargain with her. That will complete the circle.

We're so close to the ground now that I can see the steeply sloped roof of a temple. I can just make out the statues of grimacing demons on the walls, part man, part animal. It hits me how strange and exotic everything is going to be here. I've never been out of the country before. I hope I won't have any problems.

Sak is staying in America for the summer, going to summer school; I'll stay with his family when I'm not traveling around the country. One of his sisters may come with me. They'll all be meeting me at the airport.

And Bia will be with them. We have it all worked out. It'll be a little tricky at first, acting like we don't know each other. But we'll get to be friendly very soon. He's the right age for me, and he speaks English. It's only natural that he and I would start spending time together.

Bia did not just walk out the door of our house and try to make his own way back to Thailand, as he had thought he'd have to do. The day after he told his story I made the first payment on the pendant—and that night Mom and Dad decided to let him use the second half of the ticket. Dad lent him several hundred dollars as well. He promised to pay them back, and he's already sent them more than half of what he owes. He also continues to give money to his parents, so it's not easy for him. But he's doing better now.

Because of the money Dad lent him, he was able to repay his friend Chai. Loyalty to his old friend was not the only reason it was important to pay him back as soon as possible. He also didn't want to have any connection to the shady aspects of Chai's life. Not being indebted to him made it easier for Bia to keep his distance.

And because of the money from Dad, Bia didn't have to return to his old job right away. It turns out that he did work cleaning floors, though in an office building, not the post office. The little he told us about it did give credibility to the story we told Sak.

As soon as Bia got back to Thailand he brought flowers to the spirit at the Erewan Shrine; he put gold leaf on the Buddha there. Then he visited his parents, and Sak's parents too. Because he didn't have to go back to work immediately, he was able to spend some time with them. He was especially helpful to Sak's family.

And—after I'd made the second payment on the pendant—a very lucky thing happened. One of Sak's sisters had just started working as a maid in a hotel in Bangkok. She knew of an opening there, carrying luggage. Bia got the job. He did well. His English had improved after six weeks in America, and of course he had perfect manners. A few months later I made another payment—and Bia wrote that he had been promoted to bell captain. Three weeks ago I made the next to last payment. That's when they gave him a much better job, at the reception desk. He got me a very good rate at the hotel. I'll stay there after I leave Sak's family's house. We'll go sight-seeing together on his days off.

The plane is landing now—and I know that takeoffs

and landings are the most dangerous moments of a flight. I reach up to touch the Buddha pendant around my neck.

It's not there.

The plane hits the runway, bounces, and hits again, shuddering. Where is the pendant? I lean forward to look on the floor. Wind screams against the wing flaps. It's got to be here! I can't reach the floor because of the seat belt, so I feel for the pendant on the cushion and in the crack between the seats; I reach into the pocket in front of me. I can't find it.

I'm panicking now. I promised I'd give it to the spirit. Spirits must be stronger here than in America. I think of the grimacing demons I saw on the temple only moments ago. Maybe I packed the pendant in my carry-on bag. But I know I didn't. I remember touching the pendant on my neck when we landed in Tokyo.

But I don't remember touching it when we took off.

I pull my bag out from under the seat in front of me. I check through it frantically, even though I know the pendant won't be there—and it isn't. Did I lose it at the Tokyo airport, where I was so dazed? The thought bites into my stomach. I never did have a chance to get the clasp fixed; it was so loose it could easily have fallen off. And I had promised Bia I would never be careless with it!

The man next to me starts to get up, even though the seat-belt sign is still on. The cabin attendant appears instantly and tells him to sit down. "Excuse me," I say to her. "Did anybody find a pendant in the bathroom, a gold chain with a jade Buddha? I lost it. Maybe it fell off in there."

"No. I don't think so," she says. She pretends to look

concerned, her perfect eyebrows moving almost a six-teenth of an inch. "I will ask," she promises, and moves quickly away, busy and preoccupied. She has more important things to do.

The seat-belt sign goes off. I squeeze down onto my knees and reach under the seat. The pendant isn't on the floor. I push the wrong way against the crowd, into the bathroom; no pendant. It must have fallen off in there, and someone must have taken it. Or else it's in Tokyo.

I'm the last person on the plane now; they'll throw me off in a minute. The heat is sudden and fierce when I step outside. Aching with worry, I follow the other passengers down the steps to the runway. The air shimmers above the pavement. We stand sweating in a crowded bus that rumbles slowly to the terminal. I wait in line to have my passport stamped. I keep telling myself that this isn't a disaster; it just means I'll have to use almost all of my spending money to buy the spirit another pendant.

But that was the one that started the whole thing—the one Bia promised her, the one I promised to give back to her if she brought me to Thailand. That was the one she wanted. And now it's gone. How can I *help* feeling this is ominous? I think of those demons again.

Will Bia be furious? I try to assure myself that he'll be so glad to see me he'll forgive me for this. He'll know what to do; he'll tell me not to worry. Dragging my suitcase, I push through the doors to the outer terminal, where people are waiting. I look through the crowd. There are many Thai people, none of them familiar. Where's Bia? He *must* be with Sak's family.

Then I see Sak's father, his mother, the whole group. His father is holding a piece of cardboard with my name on it, but I would have recognized them anyway from the pictures Sak showed us. Suddenly I feel shy, knowing that none of them speaks English. Communicating with them isn't going to be easy.

They're not smiling, as they were in the photos. Even when I wave at them and they recognize me, their smiles are halfhearted, forced. Clearly something is wrong.

Bia isn't with them.